HAUNTINGS:

The Official
Peter Straub
Bibliography

Compiled By

Michael R.
Collings

HAUNTINGS:

The Official
Peter Straub
Bibliography

Compiled By
Michael R. Collings

Interview with Peter Straub by
Stanley Wiater

OVERLOOK CONNECTION PRESS
BILBLIO SERIES
1999

HAUNTINGS: The Official Peter Straub Bibliography
©1999 by Michael R. Collings

Interview With Peter Straub © 1999 by Stanley Wiater

Published by
Overlook Connection Press
P.O. Box 526 Woodstock GA 30188
Phone: 770-926-1762 Fax: 770-516-1469
URL: HYPERLINK http://www.overlookconnection.com
E-mail: HYPERLINK mail to:overlookcn@aol.com

Hardcover ISBN: 1-892950-15-4

Trade Paperback Edition ISBN: 1-892950-16-2

Book Design & Typesetting:
David G. Barnett/Fat Cat Design

The OCP would graciously like to thank Mr. Straub for all his assistance in putting this volume together. And especially to Dr. C. for his amazing collection of "everything Straub." Job well done, my man! —Dave

CONTENTS

The Art of Books and Other Artifacts:
An Interview In Six Parts by Stanley Wiater

7

Sections:

A. Book-length publications: Fiction, Poetry   27

B. Short Fiction: Short story, Novella   135

C. Non-Fiction: Introductions, Essays,
    Reviews, Afterwords   147

D. Poetry   155

E. Liner Note: Jazz records and CDs   165

F. Miscellaneous   169

G. Selected Secondary Sources: Interviews, Reviews,
    Articles, Biographical sketches, etc.   173

Acknowledgements   181

Index   183

THE ART OF BOOKS AND OTHER ARTIFACTS:

AN INTERVIEW IN SIX PARTS

by Stanley Wiater

To add a bit of frosting to this bibliographic cake, as it were, it was agreed by all parties that the author would be interviewed about his work from but a single viewpoint— the books *as* books. Which dust jackets did he think best represented his vision? Which covers were inappropriate to his concept of the novel? Which of his books have been most exotic or most impressive as signed/limited editions?

To better correspond to the formal bibliography, our discussion was purposely divided into six sections: trade hardcover editions, limited edition novellas, limited edition novels, poetry volumes, liner notes, and, finally, the author's thoughts on the audio adaptations of his work.

The interview was conducted on July 17, 1999, at the NECON conference in Rhode Island. To better facilitate responses from the author, every Peter Straub title the interviewer owned was spread out on the floor about us like a banquet of dark treats ready to be sampled and savored.

Section One:
First Trade Editions

Stanley Wiater: With a few of your early novels, in some situations the British edition was in fact the true first. Could you tell us which novels you believe this was the case, and also compare and contrast the artwork on the dust jackets of each?

Peter Straub: *Marriages* (1973) was first published in the U.K. by Andre Duetsch. I thought it had a very handsome jacket. The script on the jacket and the graphics were sort of like a legal document, so it looked like a marriage license. Of course, it was my first book, so I loved that jacket! *(laughs)* I thought it was beautiful.

The American jacket was okay, but a little less punchy, I think. But I liked that jacket well enough. As you can see, my name isn't very large, but then it shouldn't have been—no one had ever heard of me.

Wiater: And your feelings about *Julia*, which was published in England in 1976, a year after the American edition?

Straub: *Julia* was I believe first published in the U.K. by Jonathan Cape, as was *If You Could See Me Now*. They both had wonderful jackets—Jonathan Cape brought out *Julia* and *If You Could See Me Now* in editions that had a uniform look. That it is to say, they both had color photos on the cover. On the cover of *Julia* there was a kind of blurry photo of a young girl moving rapidly down a street. And it approximated the opening page of the book.

The cover of *If You Could See Me Now* was a candle lit image of a young girl's face looking down reflectively. That too, I thought, was very beautiful.

The American jackets don't quite come up to them. Especially *Julia*—I don't think that's very good. I really think the cover of *Julia* is an attempt to replicate something else—some other horror novel around at that time—it was a rip-off, though a mild one. When Tom Maschler, who was the head of Jonathan Cape back then, saw the American jacket of *If You Could See Me Now,* he said, Oh, I didn't know it was a *juvenile. (laughs)* That's very English— he was really sneering at it. So, those jackets are okay, but they're not terribly effective.

Wiater: With only two other exceptions—*Under Venus* and *Blue Rose*—we've purposely left out discussion of mass market paperback editions of your work. Yet we must inquire about a true oddity in your oeuvre: *Full Circle.* This is the retitled movie tie-in for a British film based on *Julia,* and one issued only in the United Kingdom. As you know, the movie was later retitled in America *The Haunting of Julia,* which still wasn't faithful to the original title of your novel. So collectors may still be confused to see the title *Full Circle* listed. How did that come about?

Straub: As happened in those days, the hardcover publisher sold the rights to a paperback house, and so I was pleased of course. But when the books came to me, and I saw...the screaming severed head of a child on the cover...I was revolted. Then at a party, held a couple of weeks later in London—we were living in England at this time—I was talking to a woman who worked in the publicity or marketing department of that very same publishing house. And I said, I have to protest: that cover is grotesque! And she said, But Peter! That book isn't for *you*! It's *not* for people like *you*. *(laughs)* Jesus! Welcome to the real world, Peter...!

Wiater: On top of that terribly lurid cover—*"a riveting, magnificently evil story of possession"*—they retitled the book as *Full Circle.*

Straub: They were trying to take full advantage, of course, of the film; a film which didn't exactly set the world on fire.

Wiater: Given the expression on your face, would you say that of all your covers, this might be the one you're least pleased with, in a general sense?

9

Straub: Oh, that *is* the one I'm least pleased with in a general—and a specific—sense.

Wiater: What are your thoughts on the jacket for *Ghost Story* (1979), which has a deceptively simple design?

Straub: In a way, the dullest of all these covers is the one on the American edition of *Ghost Story*—and yet that was very, very effective. The British edition was a painting—and I thought it was a knockout cover. But Coward, McCann & Geoghegan really didn't want to use it. They did an interesting thing though—they went to this jeweler, Angela Cummings, who worked for Tiffany's, and they had her devise a piece of jewelry that they could use as the central image for the book.

So that jeweled wasp is what she came up with—a pin. I think she only made one of them. I imagine somebody must have bought it—I only know *I* don't have it!

Wiater: There's also a simple but haunting central image on your next novel, published in 1980, *Shadowland.*

Straub: Yes, Coward, McCann & Geoghegan had done so well with the cover of *Ghost Story* that they wanted to duplicate the effect. So they went to Steuben Glass and bought this big glass owl which was used as the image on the cover. And then they had a contest to win the owl: you won the owl if you came up with the best line of ad copy.

A guy named Bruce Francis, who worked for a rare book dealer in California, came up with the line that they used in the ad and so they gave him the owl. About four years later, Bruce Francis was trying to raise money so he could become a freelance writer, and he asked me if I wanted to buy the owl. So I did—I think it was for five hundred bucks—or maybe five thousand, I forget after all this time—anyway it was an expensive tshotchy but I really liked it.

I was living in Westport, Connecticut, and I put it on a shelf or somewhere where it was always visible. When we moved later from Westport to Manhattan, it was similarly displayed. We had a wonderful cleaning woman who one day accidentally backed into the speaker it had been sitting on. It landed it on the floor, and smashed to bits. Broken hearted, I swept all the bits and put them into a paper bag and put in it the garbage.

Unbeknownst to me, my wife had found the owl's head, which was still intact. And she took it somewhere and it had it beveled and buffed so there were no sharp edges anywhere and then she gave it to me for Christmas. Now *that* was very sweet!

The English publisher used the same jacket as the American, which pretty much was the rule after that.

Wiater: Another small oddity—yet a true collectable itself—is the pack of *Shadowland* playing cards that was sent only to reviewers when the paperback edition was issued a year later.

Straub: I thought that was a cute little item to remind people of the book. The publisher of the paperback edition, Berkley Books, always claimed that they made good tshotchies. I think it's the only one ever done for my books.

Wiater: Publishers continue to use a minimum of artwork on your books. With *Floating Dragon* (1982) there's not even a central image here to describe your book; literally nothing but the evocative title and your name on a black background.

Straub: They showed me what they were going to do with the cover, which was a banner of the title on a black background. I thought that was good because I always liked the color black on dust jackets— *Mr. X* is basically black with the graphics over it. The English edition was very funny in that there's this ugly dragon's head looming over a row of suburban houses, with bare, brown mountains behind them. Mountains like you'd see in Nevada or the Sierras in California—certainly nothing like Connecticut! Clearly that artist had never been to America. Otherwise, it's a nice jacket.

Wiater: 1984's *The Talisman,* co-authored with Stephen King, followed to some degree the concept employed for *Floating Dragon*—just the title and the authors names in large print, though admittedly there is a geometric pattern spiraling in the background.

Straub: That was very straightforward. Steve said to me, "What order do you want our names in?" And I said, "Alphabetical." So on the front it says Stephen King first then Peter Straub, and on the back it says 'Peter Straub' first then 'Stephen King.' Which was nice enough.

Wiater: *Koko* was a rare instance in which the same artwork was used for both the American hardcover and the mass market paperback.

Straub: Yes, it's a computer graphic that is supposed to look like a photo. I never quite liked that image, though I like it a lot more now than I did at first. It looks like a Roualt to me, and I never really liked Roualt's paintings.

Wiater: How pleased then were you with what Dutton's art department did for *Mystery*? It's a very striking cover.

Straub: I thought *Mystery* was one of the *best* jackets I ever had.
    The U.K. edition was similar, but instead of that rose, they had a picture of a hummingbird. It was very striking, too.

Wiater: In what appears to be the only instance, the typography for your name on the cover of *Mystery* matches the typography used for your name in *Houses Without Doors*. You were a brand name, as far as the publisher was concerned.

Straub: *Houses Without Doors,* I thought, was a very good jacket, too. It's very pretty. Actually, the first image they had for the American hardback was a greenish-yellowish monster's head—and I really disliked that. So when the hardback came out, they went with the image I liked. But when the paperback came out, they put the monster's head on it!

Wiater: How did the collection entitled *Wild Animals* come about, which was also published in 1984?

Straub: *Wild Animals* was done really just as a favor to me. I suggested it to Phyllis Grann, who was then the head of Putnum, because I wanted to get this unpublished novel—*Under Venus*—into print. I'm not saying it was a great book, but it *was* readable, and I had spent a lot of time on it. And I was proud of certain parts of it; I thought it worked reasonably well, given my age and state at the time. So Phyllis Grann very kindly agreed to let me have this compendium volume along with *Julia* and *If You Could See Me Now*.

Wiater: Where did the title for the collection come from? Is it supposed to relate to any of the novels in any way?

Straub: Oh...I just made it up! I like calling collections something other than, say, *Mrs. God and other Stories*. It makes a collection tighter somehow.

Wiater: With *Under Venus,* which you wrote immediately after *Marriages*, was there ever a separate hardcover edition?

Straub: Oh, no. *Under Venus* only appeared in *Wild Animals*. Then Pocket Books—which had had a great deal of success with me—decided to put out a little run of *Under Venus* in paperback, which quickly disappeared. I have about twenty copies, which I think are all that survive—apart from yours here.

It's a nice little cover—looks kind of like a prep school novel or something like that. It even looks a little like a John Updike novel. I don't see it very often at signings—very few people ever come up with it.

Wiater: Before *The Throat* was published in 1993 there was a promotional booklet issued that some may feel is a collectable item. Was a published excerpt ever done for any of your other novels?

Straub: No. The marketing department decided to publish this little teaser which was done for the ABA and which of course was also sent out to booksellers. I don't know if it ever excited or teased anybody's interest.

Wiater: For some time you have had the good fortune to have the art departments of various publishers consult you about the dust jackets, even if they weren't contractually bound to do so.

Straub: Yes, that's usually been the case, but *The Hellfire Club* (1996) was a long battle. They solicited about a dozen individuals who did dust jackets, and none of them were any good. They went through that process for a second time, and they narrowed it down to about four choices. And I didn't really like any of them—my editor only liked one. We eventually came up with a modified image that I liked a lot at the time, but which other people told me they thought hurt the sales of the book. People told me that picture was somehow too dignified, too literary for the book itself. But I've always liked this dust jacket, though I guess a lot of other people didn't.

Wiater: With all due respect, one doesn't need a magnifying glass to find your name on the cover.

Straub: Oh—by that time I kind of expected that. *(smiles)* I was completely spoiled...! Actually, after a certain point in their careers, most writers will want that—they want their name in nice big print on the front of the book. I'm no exception...! Sometimes I think I'm so silly that I'd like *any* dust jacket if my name was big enough. There's undeniably a narcissistic satisfaction in that aspect of it.

Wiater: Speaking of spoiled, how pleased were you with your first paperback original anthology—*Peter Straub's Ghosts*, done in 1995 on behalf of the Horror Writers Association?

Straub: I thought it was cheesy—as a matter of fact, everything about it was cheesy. Pocket Books never consulted with me about *anything*—and they didn't even tell me the book was out. They never even sent me a copy! I first learned it was out when my daughter came home from high school one day and said, "Daddy, I went into the bookstore and saw this title...what's *Peter Straub's Ghosts*?"

That was the first I had heard it was published!

So I went out and bought one.

I thought the cover art looked tacky, and I thought the cover copy was also tacky—there was some very unfortunate metaphor having to do with taste or flavor—whatever it was, it really *was* in poor taste.

Wiater: Moving on to your most recent novel, *Mr. X,* published in 1999. Again only a stark title and your name on an equally stark black background.

Straub: I really like it. The only thing I asked them to change was the font in which my name was printed. It looked like my name had been done in stencils, and it reminded me of the names you see on ammo cases or on soldier's uniforms. I didn't feel that association was very appropriate to this book. So I asked them to reset my name another way, and now it looks much better. I really like the effect used on *Mr.* because it looks like Jack the Ripper's handwriting. There's something slightly crazy about that script...

Wiater: Actually, both *Mr.* and *X* are done in slightly crazy scripts. The one sane script to balance or break up to the two insane scripts is the one for your name.

Straub: Yeah, that's right. *(laughs)* That's very good.

Wiater: Speaking of something that doesn't quite exist as we speak, can you tell us how your forthcoming collection *Magic Terror* (2000) came about?

Straub: It was very much the same situation as my deciding to do *Houses Without Doors.* I looked over all the stories that I had published in anthologies, and I realized they added up to a good-sized collection. So I played with them a little, and I rearranged the contents until they were in some kind of order, and I gave it to my agent, David Gernert, and asked him to take it to Random House. And they accepted it immediately.

My daughter hates the title, by the way—she thinks it sounds like a video game. She tells me no one will buy a book with a name like *Magic Terror.* So we'll see!

Section Two:
Limited Editions-
Novellas

Wiater: How did the Donald M. Grant edition of *The General's Wife* come about in 1982?

Straub: Don Grant wrote me and asked if I had anything suitable—and short!—and I had just excised that section of what is now called *The General's Wife* out of *Floating Dragon*.

My editor, Bill Thompson, had just read the manuscript and said, Peter, it's just great except for one thing—we have to take out that section about Patsy in London. It doesn't go anywhere and it doesn't fit the rest of the book, so there's no point in having it in. So I cheerfully cut it out—and even more cheerfully retyped it and sent it on to Donald Grant when he asked for something. Along with a long introduction that he asked me to write. That book is a gorgeous little object.

The story originally appeared in an issue of the now defunct *Rod Serling's The Twilight Zone Magazine*, and then there's this limited edition—and that's all there'll ever be.

Wiater: What about the Underwood-Miller edition of *Blue Rose*, which appeared in 1985? Were you pleased with how that came out?

Straub: I was more than pleased, I was delighted with what Underwood-Miller had done with the book. Ned Dameron did a great painting of a ghastly, toxic blue rose for the jacket, Pendragon Graphics designed the book beautifully, and it came in a slipcase wrapped in some soft, smooth fabric. It was a really striking, and strikingly well done, production.

Wiater: *Blue Rose* also appeared once more in a special edition, didn't it? That was when Penguin Books, to celebrate its 60th anniversary as a publisher, chose sixty authors from which to issue sixty unique paperback editions.

Straub: Yes, that was really sweet. Those were true "pocket books," in that you could literally slip them into your shirt pocket. And they sold them for ninety-five cents! It was a charming idea. I love the fact that I was included in that number—very few living authors were included. They had a spectacular list of titles.

Wiater: In 1990, Donald M. Grant did a limited edition of your novella, *Mrs. God*.

Straub: He did a very beautiful job on that, too. Rick Berry did a great job on the illustrations, which were haunting. And evocative. Rick called me up and said, "What sort of look do you like?" And I said, "Well, what I have in mind in certain points during that book were paintings by Rousseau—there's one of a woman...playing a flute against a lush tropical background. That's the sort of feeling I want." And he said, "That's all I have to know." And he was off and running.

Section Three: Limited Editions- Novels

Wiater: Borderlands Press did limited editions of both your HWA anthology *Ghosts* and *The Throat*.

Straub: Both were great. *The Throat* was done in a very, very handsome edition with a nice painting by an artist named Ryan Driemiller. He did a knockout job.

Wiater: In 1985, Hill House did the limited of *Ghost Story*, with illustrations by Stephen Gervais. Did you consult with the artist in this instance?

Straub: Steve Gervais did very nice illustrations for that. But I don't think we talked about them beforehand. I remember meeting him for the first time at a convention and he showed me certain drawings that he had done. I was very impressed by them. I bought a little painting he'd done that referred to *Shadowland*...a tree with lights in its leaves. I thought that was a very nice painting—though it was very small, about the size of a postcard.

Wiater: You did another limited with Underwood-Miller in 1982, this time with *Floating Dragon*.

Straub: It was hell of a job! Leo and Diane Dillon—whom I didn't know then—did a beautiful painting of a bouquet of flowers that gets more corrupt and sinister the more you look at it. Later, through another set of people, we came to know the Dillons, and now we see Leo and Diane all the time! I wish I could figure out a way that they could illustrate another one of my books, but they're *very* busy. They're fantastic people.

Wiater: Perhaps the most elaborate of the limited editions to date would be Donald M. Grant's three distinct versions of *The Talisman*, all of which were issued simultaneously in 1985?

Straub: Now—talk about knockout jobs! *(laughs)* All were beautiful—but they got more and more beautiful as the number the print runs got smaller and smaller. So the one that's signed by everybody—all seventy copies!—is absolutely gorgeous!! Seventy copies! I think Grant gave me about ten of them.

And I *gave* most of them away...! I think I might have one or two left. I just hope the people I gave them to appreciate it; now I wish I could remember who they are...!

Wiater: In 1995 Gauntlet Press did an elaborate limited of *Shadowland* with a foreword by Ramsey Campbell and an afterword by Thomas Tessier. Your thoughts on doing a limited fifteen years after it was first published?

Straub: Publisher Barry Hoffman originally wanted to do *Ghost Story*, but then I told him that Hill House had already done a limited, so he suggested *Shadowland*. It's a very handsome book, and Harry O. Morris jacket is gorgeous. The whole production is very, very handsome.

Wiater: You mentioned earlier how they had made wonderful gifts, what does it mean to you as an author to see your book issued in a run of just a few hundred exquisitely produced copies?

Straub: You've hit on a good point—because they *do* make very nice gifts. People may not always enjoy getting them, but at least they pretend that they are delighted to get them! But the value for me as an author is as an *objet d art*: they are simply very handsome objects.

I don't have any particular favorites, as they're all great in their own way. I do wish *Ghost Story* had been reset, instead of using the original plates from the trade edition, so that one isn't quite as special as the others. And I think the publisher, Peter Schneider, feels the same, because he told me he regretted having to use the same plates. Why that was done I can't recall, though it may be have been for budgetary reasons.

Section Four: Poetry

Wiater: Would you consider your earliest volumes of poetry, such as *My Life In Pictures*, which appeared back in 1971, as amongst your rarest works?

Straub: The rarest would have to be the first one of all, when Thomas Tessier and I published a little series of six pamphlets we called Seafront Press. We did a little pamphlet of his, a little pamphlet of mine, one of a friend of ours named Tom Redshawe, one by a poet named Grace Schulman, and I forget who else at the moment.

Anyway, mine was a single poem called *My Life In Pictures*, and for my 40th birthday, Thomas Tessier produced a copy. I'd lost mine years before! He must have had two of them.

So I now have *one* copy—which I think is about as rare as you can get.

Wiater: What about *Ishmael,* which appeared in a signed numbered edition of 100 copies in 1972, when you were still living in England?

Straub: That was published by Turret Books. At the time, it cost about a quarter. I see it in rare book catalogs now and then for about $350.00 bucks.

I believe I have two copies.

Wiater: *Open Air* was issued by a Press in Dublin, also in 1972. It's a collection of nineteen poems.

Straub: *Open Air* was published by Irish University Press. After a couple of years—make that ten years—the publisher wanted to get rid of his back stock, so he sent me all the copies he had. Several boxes of *Open Air* sat in my garage in Westport for about five or six years, and now what's left of them are sitting in my basement in New York. I believe there were 500 copies printed, and so I must have had 200 when I first got the boxes. I gave a whole bunch away so I might only have about 50 or 60 left.

There were also 100 copies of a hardcover edition. I don't believe there's any image at all on the cover; it just has the title on the spine, as it does on the paperback. It was a very handsome book, with a gray fabric.

Wiater: Easily the most elaborate of your poetry collections would have to be *Leeson Park and Belsize Square*, which appeared in 1983 from Underwood-Miller in a hardcover edition of a thousand copies in three distinct states.

Straub: Underwood-Miller knocked themselves out with *Leeson Park and Belsize Square*. Though in my opinion they slightly *overdid* it. For example, I don't know why that picture of the cathedral is on the cover. I also don't like this medieval-looking typeface here that the title is done in—and I don't like that red color. The title just gets *lost*. In fact, it's too busy for any words to be clearly read. However—the interior of the book is really handsomely done.

Wiater: Would you consider this volume, if we're not stretching the term too far, your collected poems?

Straub: It doesn't have *everything* in it...but I guess you could call it that. Though then it's an awfully small collected poems.

Wiater: The reason for the question is because there might be still be uncollected poems written since the publication of that volume?

Straub: No, that just went away. After I wrote prose day after day after day for a couple of years I couldn't write short lines anymore. And that's just what happened with *Leeson Park and Belsize Square,* in that it gradually but inexorably progresses towards prose poetry.

Wiater: You mentioned the Seafront Press as being the publisher of your very first published work. Is it safe to assume this name eventually transformed into the Seafront Corporation for use on your copyright notices?

Straub: Yes, that's where I got the name from. I probably owe Tessier half of everything I've ever earned. *(laughs)*

Tessier and I were walking down a street in Dublin, and we were trying to think of a name for our little project—which didn't go very far—and he stopped on one particular square of pavement and said, "How about Seafront?" And I said, "That's really good." Then he pointed down to the pavement and said, "Twenty years from now we'll come back here and say this is where we made that up!"

Wiater: And...?

Straub: No, we didn't return. But on the other hand, Seafront lives, in a sense.

Section Five:
Liner Notes
for Jazz Albums

Wiater: How in the world did you get involved in writing liner notes for jazz albums?

Straub: My secret sideline! *(laughs)* I always wanted to know jazz musicians, and then I got to know a whole bunch of them. Two of them became my very good friends—Scott Hamilton and Warren Vache—and later on I got to know Phil Woods, who's a great, great alto player. And Tommy Flanagan, who's a heroic, legendary bebop piano player—and is a neighbor of mine. I think one day Scott asked me if I would do the liner notes for a CD of his, and by this time I was going to most of his recording dates, and just hanging out in the studio while he and his band recorded tracks.

So I was inside the process, in a matter of speaking.

It was fun to write the notes, because Scott and I had similar interests, and there were certain things I wanted to explore or express about the way he played. After that, the president of Concord Records, Carl Jefferson (who is now deceased), asked me to do some notes because he saw me all the time in the studio and knew—vaguely—that I was a writer. After that Scott asked me to do some, and then Warren asked me to do a couple, and Phil Woods asked me to do some—and then other people I had met through them *also* asked me, because they liked the way I wrote.

Pretty soon I had written fifteen or twenty liner notes.

It got harder as I went along because—technically—I don't know anything about music and I was in danger of exhausting whatever I had to say about the subject. I think I'm about done doing liner notes…though I find it very hard to say no.

Section Six:
Audio Books

Wiater: You've had a fair number of works adapted to the audio book format, which is wonderful. On the other hand, they've all been abridged, which is certainly less than perfection for an author.

Straub: They've all been abridged, for sure. With the possible exception of *Mrs. God,* which I believe is unabridged. I *like* audio books...yet sometimes they really do violence to a work because they take so much out! *The Throat* particularly suffered from that, even though I think it's four cassettes. I think *Mr. X* might be six cassettes.

But still, what the listener gets is about ninety pages of text. And that's out of seven or eight hundred pages of text.

Wiater: If they're always less than perfect in terms of being abridged, why do you authorize audio versions to be done?

Straub: Well, a *lot* of people like audio books. And they're fun to listen to, I think. I'm pleased to have had great actors like William H. Macy, and James Woods, and Kevin Spacey read my books. The adapters work very hard to do it right. Most of them consult me and ask if there's anything I would suggest that they definitely *not* take out.

Wiater: Any likelihood of any of your novels being done in unabridged versions?

Straub: I believe a couple have been done unabridged as Books for the Blind. Which means they must be like twenty tapes, and some poor soul must sit there in a studio all day long for weeks and weeks reading into a mike. I've never seen any of them, but I know it happened, because I gave permission.

You don't get any money for that, of course, but on the other hand morally I'm glad it's been done.

* * * * *

An award winning journalist, Stanley Wiater has, according to *Hauntings: The Official Peter Straub Bibliography*, interviewed the author more than other writer. His first interview with Straub was conducted in 1979.

A.

Book-length publications– Fiction, Poetry

A1.

My Life In Pictures

(1971)

A1. *MY LIFE IN PICTURES*. Dublin: Seafront Press, 1971, 4 pp., 10 pence, stapled pamphlet. Poetry. [see D1]

COMMENTS: The pamphlet consists of the title poem, without a contents page. Straub notes further that "Seafront Press was begun by Thomas Tessier and myself in that year [1971], and we published six pamphlets altogether."

ISHMAEL

PETER STRAUB

ISHMAEL. London: Turret Books, 1972.

A2.

Ishmael (1972)

A2. *Ishmael.* London: Turret Books, 1972, 21 pp., £3.15; signed, numbered edition of 100 copies. Turret Booklet, Second series, Number 14. ISBN 0854690379. Poetry.

    b. Excerpted in: *A Fantasy Reader: The Seventh World Fantasy Convention Book.* Edited by Jeff Frane and Jack Rems. Berkeley CA: Seventh World Fantasy Convention, 1981. Collection of fiction and non-fiction by Straub, Stephen King, Dennis Etchison, Ray Bradbury, and others.

CONTENTS: "The First Bedouin" [see D7]; "The Desert Motion" [see D2]; "Ishmael's Song to His Sister" [see D8]; "The Bow" [see D3]; "Using the Bow" [see D4]; "Ishmael in Manhattan" [see D9]; "Downtown, Way Down" [see D10]; "The Music He Hears" [see D11]; "The Sleepers" [see D5]; "Song for One on Water" [D12]; "A Loosening, A Spending Prose" [see D13]; "From Lawrence's Letters" [see D14]; "On Hampstead Heath with Women" [see D6]; "Envoi from a Brother" [see D15]

OPEN AIR. Dublin [Shannon], Ireland: Irish University Press, 1972.

A3.

Open Air (1972)

A3. *OPEN AIR.* Dublin [Shannon], Ireland: Irish University Press, 1972, 47 pp. Signed, numbered casebound edition of 100 copies. ISBN 0-7165-2176-8. Poetry collection.

    b. Dublin, Ireland: Irish University Press, 1972, 47 pp., £1.25, paperback; signed, numbered casebound edition of 500 copies in wrappers. ISBN 0-7165-217-5.

CONTENTS:

    FOX: "Fox Survives" [see D16]; "Fox in Snow" [see D17]; "Circling the Ground" [see D18]; "Tracking" [see D19]; "Fox Reading" [see D20]; "Fox's Address to the Delegates" [see D21]; "Fox's Arrogance" [see D22]; "Fox by the Pool" [see D23]; "Explications" [see D24]

    WOLF: "Wolf on the Plains" [see D25]; "Words from the Island" [see D26]; "Muhammed's Song" [see D27]; "Wolf's Litany" [see D28]; "Wolf and the Territory" [see D29]; "Preparations for Dying" [see D30]; "Isobel's Recitative" [see D31]; "After the Return" [see D32]; "The Blessing" [see D33]

    FISH: "Coming to One" [see D34]

COMMENTS: All copies are identified as "First Edition 1972."

SELECTED ARTICLES AND REVIEWS:

1. "The State of Ireland." *Times Literary Supplement* No. 3702 (16 February 1973): 183. Straub "writes a poetry of assured, slow-moving, resonant statement, which is at best potent and at worse ponderous. Technically he is extremely competent, well able to exploit (sometimes over-consciously) dramatic shifts and pauses, working for the most part in drastically cramped and abbreviated units but capable, too, of some expansive imaginative flights."

MARRIAGES. New York: Coward, McCann & Geoghegan, 1973.

A4.

Marriages (1973)

A4. *MARRIAGES*. London: Andre Deutsch, 1973, 234 pp., £2.25, hard-cover, 3,000 copies. ISBN 0233963847. Novel.

    b. New York: Coward, McCann & Geoghegan, 1973, 234 pp., $5.95, hardcover, 7,000 copies. ISBN 0698104862.

    c. New York: Pocket Books, July 1977, 260 pp., $1.75, paper. ISBN 0-671-8276-9.

    d. As: *Die Fremde Frau* ['The Strange Woman']. München, Germany: Wilhelm Heyne Verlag, 1987, 285 pp., DM 6,80, paperback. German translation by Joachim Körber. ISBN 3-453-00292-X..

    e. As: *Die Fremde Frau* ['The Strange Woman']. München, Germany: Wilhelm Heyne Verlag, HEYNE ALLGEMEINE RIEHE #10071, 1997, 285 pp., DM 12,90, paperback. ISBN 3-453-11669-0.

SELECTED ARTICLES AND REVIEWS:

1. *Best Sellers* Vol. 33 (1 May 1973): 56.
2. *Books & Bookmen* Vol. 18 (May 1973): 100.
3. Bryden, Ronald. "American Scenes." *The Listener* Vol. 89, No. 2294 (March 15, 1973): 348. "Where Straub shows himself a real writer is in evoking the shallow foreground and aftermath to love's exaltations...."
4. *Esquire* Vol. 79 (May 1973): 68.
5. *Kirkus Review* Vol. 41 (15 January 1973): 80.
6. Levin, Martin. "New & Novel." *New York Times Book Review* (18 March 1973): 40.
7. *Library Journal* Vol. 98 (15 April 1973): 1310.
8. "Poet's Prose." *Times Literary Supplement* No. 3707 (23 March 1973): 313. "Mr Straub ... is what is commonly called a 'poetic novelist', with the fine sense of the weight of words which every novelist should have, and which many poets lack."
9. *Publishers Weekly* Vol. 203 (5 February 1973): 82.
10. Ridge, Putney Tyson, Ph.D. (pseudonym for Straub). "Marriages." Available at: http://www.net-site.com/straub/put_mar.htm.

A NOVEL BY
PETER
STRAUB

MARRIAGES. London: Andre Deutsch, 1973.

JULIA. New York: Coward, McCann & Geoghegan, 1975.

A5.
Julia *(1975)*

A5. *JULIA.* New York: Coward, McCann & Geoghegan, 1975, 287 pp., $7.95, hardcover edition of [about] 15,000 copies. ISBN 0-698-10695-4. Novel.

b. London: Jonathan Cape, 1976, 287 pp., £2.95, hardcover. ISBN 0-224-01191-X.

c. As: *Julia.* Helsinki, Finland: Weilin+Göös, 1975, 308 pp., hardcover. Finnish translation by Marja Heinonen. ISBN 951-638-126-X.

d. New York: Pocket Books, 1976, 294 pp., $3.50, mass market paperback. ISBN 0-671-45283-5.

e. New York: Pocket Books, October 1976, 255 pp., $1.95, mass-market paperback. ISBN 0-671-80751-X. Also published as: ISBN 0-671-82649-2. 19th printing by 1999.

f. As: *Full Circle.* London: Corgi, 1977, 253 pp., 85p, trade paper. ISBN 0-552-10471-X.

g. As: *Julia.* Stockholm, Sweden: Norstedt, 1977, 241 pp., 72:00 SEK (Swedish Kronor), hardcover. Swedish translation by Annika Preis. ISBN 9117710022.

h. As: *Julia.* Helsinki, Finland: Weilin+Göös, 1977. Finnish translation by Marja Heinonen.

i. As: *Julia.* Helsinki, Finland: Uusi Kirjakerho [New Book-Club], 1977.

j. New York: Pocket Books, February 1979, 255 pp., $5.99, mass-market paperback. ISBN 0-671-73468-7. Reprinted 1984, 1990.

k. As *Julia.* Paris, France: Éditions Seghers, 1979, 278 pp., 58 F, hardcover. French translation by Franck Straschitz.

l. As: *La Obsesión de Julia* ['The Obsession of Julia']. __: Aims International Books, September 1985, $9.95, paperback. Spanish translation. ISBN 8401321344.

m. As: *La Obsesión de Julia* ['The Obsession of Julia']. Esplugues de Llobregat (Barcelona, Spain): Plaza & Janes, S.A., PLAZA &

JANES ÉXITOS, November 1985, 272 pp., 873 pta, paperback. Spanish translation by J. Ferrer Aleu. ISBN 84-01-32134-4.

n. As: *Cuando el Circulo se Cierra* ['When the Circle Closes Itself']. Barcelona, Spain: Bruguera, BRUGUERA CINCO ESTRELLAS #126, February 1985, 368 pp., 700 pta., paperback. Spanish translation by Jordi Pratmasó Soldevila 84-02-10335-9.

o. As: *Julia.* München, Germany: Wilhelm Heyne Verlag, HEYNE ALLGEMEINE REIHE #01/6724, 1986, 318 pp., DM 7,80, paperback. German translation by Joachim Körber. ISBN 3-453-02328-5.

p. As: *Full Circle.* London: Corgi, January 1987, 254 pp., £2.50, paperback reissue. 0-552-10471-X.

q. As: *Le cercle inferna* ['The Hellish Circle"]. Paris, France: NéO Plus, #18, January 1988, 278 pp., 96 FF., hardcover. French translation by Franck Straschitz. Illustrated by Jean-Michel Nicollet. ISBN 2-7304-0499-6.

r. As: *Julia.* Paris, France: Presses Pocket, TERREUR #9020, November 1989, 283 pp., 28.00 FF/3.96 Euro, paperback. French translation by Franck Straschitz. Illustrated by Marc Demoulin. ISBN 2-266-03181-3.

s. As: *Duivelsbroed* ['Devilish Brood']. Amsterdam, Netherlands: Uitgeverij Luitingh-Sijthoff, 1990, 240 pp., paperback. Dutch translation. ISBN 90-245-1656-0.

t. As: *La Obsesión de Julia* ['The Obsession of Julia']. Esplugues de Llobregat (Barcelona, Spain): Plaza & Janés, S.A., LOS JET DE PLAZA & JANÉS #110, July 1991, 256 pp., 558 pta, paperback. Spanish translation by J. Ferrer Aleu. ISBN 84-01-49110-X.

u. As: *La Obsesión de Julia* ['The Obsession of Julia']. Esplugues de Llobregat (Barcelona, Spain): Plaza & Janés, S.A., LOS JET DE PLAZA & JANÉS #160/BIBLIOTECA DE PETER STRAUB #4, July 1993, 256 pp., 801 pta, paperback. Spanish translation by J. Ferrer Aleu. ISBN 84-01-49424-9.

v. As: *Julia.* Finland: Gummerus, 1993, 308 pp., hardcover. Finnish translation by Marja Heinonen. ISBN 951-20-4353-X.

w. As: *Julia.* Milano, Italy: Bompiani, 1993, 246 pp., 12 L, paperback. Italian translation by Olivia Crosio. ISBN 88-452-2069-9.

x. As: *Julia.* Poznan, Poland: Dom Wydawniczy Rebis, 1994, 283 pp., paperback. Polish translation by Aleksander Gomola. ISBN 83-7120-055-2.

y. As: *Julia*. München, Germany: Wilhelm Heyne Verlag, HEYNE ALLGEMEINE REIHE #10305, July 1997, 318 pp., DM 12,90; paperback. German translation by Joachim Körber. ISBN 3-453-12475-8.

z. As: *Julie*. Czech Republic: Aurora, 1997, 221 pp., 189 CZK, hardcover. Czech translation by Jiri Janra; cover art by Michal Houba. ISBN 80-85974-35-5.

aa. As: *Full Circle*. Film, 1976. Fetter Productions (UK) and Classic Film Industries (Canada). Producers: Peter Fetterman and Alfred Pariser. Executive Producer: Julian Melzack. Director: Richard Loncraine. Screenplay: Dave Humphries, based on adaptation by Harry Bromley Davenport. Cast: Mia Farrow, Keir Dullea, Tom Conti, Robin Gammell, Jill Bennet, Cathleen Nesbitt.

COMMENTS: *Julia* was the first of Straub's novels for which an advance uncorrected proof was published; all of his subsequent novels have had such proofs.

SELECTED ARTICLES AND REVIEWS:
1. *Best Sellers* Vol. 35 (November 1975): 238.
2. Cunningham, Valentine. *The New Statesman* Vol. 91 (27 February 1976): 264.
3. Gordon, James. "Demonic Children." *New York Times Book Review* 11 September 1977: 3, 52. Brief mention of *Julia* in a psychological study of aggressive children in American horror fiction.
4. *Kirkus Reviews* Vol. 43 (1 August 1975): 874.
5. Lucas, Tim, and Contributing Editors of *Video Times Magazine*. "*Haunting of Julia, The.*" *Your Movie Guide to Horror Video Tapes and Discs*. Publications International, 1985. 59-60. Review of film version.
6. Mason, Michael. "Nasty and Nastier." *Times Literary Supplement* No. 3859 (February 27, 1976): 213.
7. Mellors, John. "Kensington Gore." *The Listener* Vol. 95, No. 2446 (February 26, 1976): 254.
8. Neilson, Keith. "Julia." *Horror Literature: A Reader's Guide*. Edited by Neil Barron. New York: Garland, 1990. 304.
9. *New Statesmen & Society* Vol. 3 (7 December 1990): 34. Review of *Full Circle*.
10. *Observer* [London] 29 February 1976:27.

11. *Publishers Weekly* Vol. 208 (1 September 1975): 69.
12. *Publishers Weekly* Vol. 210 (13 September 1976): 98.
13. Ridge, Putney Tyson, Ph.D. (pseudonym for Straub). *"Julia."* Online: http://net-site.com/straub/put_jul.htm.
14. *School Library Journal* Vol. 22 (December 1975): 33.
15. *School Library Journal* Vol. 22 (October 1975): 112.
16. Schulman, Madeline G. *Library Journal* Vol. 100 (15 October 1975): 1950. "Some scenes are deliberately nauseating, and since evil triumphs completely, the resolution of the story is unpleasant, but there is an audience for this type of book."
17. *Spectator* Vol. 236 (28 February 1976): 22.
18. *Village Voices Literary Supplement* (May 1993): 25+.

JULIA. London: Jonathan Cape, 1975.

IF YOU COULD SEE ME NOW. New York: Coward, McCann & Geoghegan, June 1977.

A6.

If You Could See Me Now (1977)

A6. *IF YOU COULD SEE ME NOW.* London: Jonathan Cape, June 1977, 287 p., £3.95, hardcover; 7,000 copies. ISBN 0-224-01345-9. Novel.

   b. New York: Coward, McCann & Geoghegan, June 1977, 287 pp., $8.95, hardcover. Flyleaf reads: "First American Edition." ISBN 0-698-10817-5.

   c. London: Futura, 1978, 287 pp., 90p, mass-market paperback. ISBN 0-7088-1379-8.

   d. New York: Pocket Books, February 1979, 328 pp., $2.75, mass-market paperback. ISBN 0-671-41052-0. Also as: New York: Pocket Books, 1979, 328 pp., $3.50, mass-market paperback. ISBN 0-671-45193-6.

   e. As: *Wenn du Wüsstest...*['If You Knew…']. Wien [Vienna], Austria: Paul Zsolnay Verlag, August 1979, 404 pp. German translation by Elizabeth Hartweger. ISBN 0-385-23941-6.

   f. As: *Wenn du Wüsstest...*['If You Knew…']. Hamburg, Germany, Zsolnay, 1979, 405 pp., hardcover. German translation by Elisabeth Hartweger. ISBN 3-552-03133-2.

   g. As: *Si pudieras verme ahora* ['If You Could See Me Now']. Barcelona, Spain: Bruguera, BRUGUERA CINCO ESTRELLAS #119, October 1984, 384 pp., 975 pta, paperback. Spanish translation by Hernán Sabaté Vargas. ISBN 84-02-09325-6.

   h. New York: Pocket Books, January 1986, 328 pp., $3.95, paperback reissue. ISBN 0-671-50633-1. 7th printing.

   i. As: *Si Pudieras Verme Ahora* ['If You Could See Me Now']. Barcelona, Spain: Plaza & Janés Editores, PLAZA & JANÉS ÉXITOS, June 1986, December 1986, 256 pp., 1179 pta, trade paperback. Spanish translation by Adolfo Martín. ISBN 84-01-

3219-13.

j. As: *Si pudieras verme ahora* ['If You Could See Me Now']. Barcelona, Spain: Círculo de Lectores, S.A., September 1987, 296 pp., 873 pta, hardcover. Spanish translation by Adolfo Martín. ISBN 84-226-2345-5.

k. New York: Pocket Books, 1990, $6.99, mass-market paperback reprint. ISBN 0-671-73467-9.

l. As: *Tu as beaucoup changé, Alison* ['You/Thou Have Altered Greatly, Alison']. Paris, France: Editions J'ai Lu, ÉPOUVANTE #2816, May 1990, 414 pp., 37FF, paperback. French translation by Jean-Paul Martin. Illustrated by Franco Accornero. ISBN 2-277-22816-8.

m. As: *Si Pudieras Verme Ahora* ['If You Could See Me Now']. Barcelona: Plaza & Janés Editores, LOS JET DE PLAZA & JANÉS #160/BIBLIOTECA DE PETER STRAUB #2, June 1991, 320 pp., 728 pta, paperback. Spanish translation by Adolfo Martín. ISBN 84-01-49422-2.

n. As: *Draaikolk* ['Whirlpool']. Utrecht, Netherlands: Uitgeverij Luitingh, 1991, 303 pp., paperback. ISBN 90-245-1719-2.

o. As: *Patto di Sangue* ["Pact of Blood"]. Milano, Italy: Armenia Editore, 1991, 283pp., trade paperback. ISBN 88-344-0470-X.

p. As: *Patto di Sangue* ["Pact of Blood"]. Milano, Italy: Armenia Editore, 1993, 283pp., hardcover.

q. As: *Jos näkisit minut* ["If You Could See Me"]. Helsinki, Finland: Book Studio Oy, 1992, 314 pp., paperback. Finnish translation by Kari Salminem. ISBN 951-611-470-9.

r. As: *Wenn du Wüsstest...* ['If You Knew...']. München, Germany: Wilhelm Heyne Verlag, 1994, 383 pp., DM 12,90; paperback. German translation by Elisabeth Hartweger. ISBN 3-453-03330-2.

s. As: *Wenn du Wüsstest...* ['If You Knew...']. München, Germany: DTV, 1995, 392 pp., DM 14,90; trade paperback. German translation by Elisabeth Hartweger. ISBN 3-423-12052-5.

t. As: *Wenn du Wüsstest...* ['If You Knew...']. München, Germany: DTV, 1997, 427 pp., DM 10,00; paperback. German translation by Elisabeth Hartweger. ISBN 3-423-08373-5.

u. As audiotape: Listen for Pleasure, Inc., November 1986, $16.99, abridged, 2 cassettes. Read by Keir Dullea. ISBN 0-886-46166-9.

SELECTED ARTICLES AND REVIEWS:

1. Ackroyd, Peter. "Vasty Deep." *The Spectator* Vol. 239, No. 7774 (July 9, 1977): 234. "The book quite carefully evokes the real world of everyday folk, while at the same time intimating—through dreams, metaphors and analogies—the existence of a superior reality which can occasionally be understood."
2. Casey, Carol K. *Library Journal* Vol. 102 (1 May 1977): 1045. "Straub has written a superb follow-up to his recent bestseller, *Julia*....Straub once again combines the natural and supernatural for maximum effect and almost unbearable suspense."
3. Keates, Jonathan. "Furtively Twitching." *New Statesman* Vol. 93, No. 2414 (June 24, 1977): 863. "Crisp, classy buggaboo, this, full of neatly managed understatements and chillingly calculated surprises."
4. *Kirkus Reviews* Vol. 45 (1 April 1977): 379.
5. *Kliatt Young Adult Paperback Book Guide* Vol. 27 (July 1993): 48+. Review of audio version.
6. Neilson, Keith. "If You Could See Me Now." *Horror Literature: A Reader's Guide.* Edited by Neil Barron. New York: Garland, 1990. 303. "*If You Could See Me Now* is a strong horror novel—subtle, complex, intense."
7. *Observer* [London] 3 July 1977: 24.
8. *Publishers Weekly* Vol. 211 (28 March 1977): 76.
9. *Publishers Weekly* Vol. 214 (11 December 1978): 68.
10. Ridge, Putney Tyson, Ph.D., (pseudonym for Straub). "*If You could See Me Now*." Online: http://net-site.com/straub/pt_ifyou.htm.
11. Ryan, John. "Trouble in Arden." *Times Literary Supplement* 12 August 1977: 989. "*If You Could See Me Now* is no run-of-the-mill post-Freudian ghost story....[its] ironic literary underlay deepens rather than diminishes the fear."
12. *Village Voice Literary Supplement* (May 1993): 25+.

IF YOU COULD SEE ME NOW. London: Jonathan Cape, June 1977.

GHOST STORY. New York: Coward, McCann & Geoghegan, April 1979.

A7.
Ghost Story *(1979)*

A7. GHOST STORY. London: Jonathan Cape, 1979, 483 pp., $10.95, hardcover; 15,000 copies. ISBN 0698109597. Novel. Also: 507 pp., hardcover; ISBN 0-224-01686-5.

    b. New York: Coward, McCann & Geoghegan, April 1979, 483 pp., $10.95, hardcover; 50,000 copies. First American Edition; flyleaf reads: "First Edition." ISBN 698-10959-7.

    c. As: *Le Fantôme de Milburn* ['The Ghost of Milburn']. Paris, France: Seghers, January 1979, 432 pp., 58 FF, hardcover. French translation by Frank Straschitz. Preface by François Rivière.

    d. New York: Coward, McCann & Geoghegan, [1979?], 483 pp., hardcover. Book Club Edition. No ISBN.

    e. London: Futura, 1979, 507 pp., paperback. ISBN 0-7088-1604-5.

    f. As: *Kummitusjuttu* ['Ghost-Tale']. Finland: Kirjayhtymä ['Book-Concern'], 1979. Finnish translation by Matti Kannosto.

    g. As: *Kummitusjuttu* ['Ghost-Tale']. Finland: Uusi Kirjakerho [New Book-Club], 1979. Finnish translation by Matti Kannosto.

    h. New York: Pocket Books, 1980, 567 pp., paperback. ISBN 0-671-68563-5. 28th printing by 1999.

    i. As: *Fantasmus* ['Ghosts']. Spain, 1980, paperback. Spanish translation. ISBN 9997768086.

    j. As: *Gengångare* ['Ghost']. Stockholm, Sweden: Norstedt, 1980, 443 pp., 125:00 SEK (Swedish Kronor), hardcover. Swedish translation by Astrid Lundgren. ISBN 9118020127.

k. *Fantasmas* ['Ghosts']. Barcelona, Spain: Bruguera, BRUGUERA CINCO ESTRELLAS #68, October 1981, 416 pp., 675 pta, paperback. Spanish translation by Lucrecia Moreno de Saenz. ISBN 84-02-08270-X.

l. As: *Geisterstunde* ["Hour of Ghosts"]. München, Germany: Der Goldmann Verlag, 1981, 599 pp., DM 10,00; paperback. German translation by Hanna Molden. ISBN 3-442-11969-3.

m. As: *Geisterstunde* ["Hour of Ghosts"]. München, Germany: Verlag Fritz Molden, 1981, 544 pp.; hardcover. German translation by Hanna Molden. ISBN 3-217-01036-1.

n. As: *Fantasmas* ['Ghosts']. __: Ediciones Forum, S.A., BIBLIOTECA DEL TERROR, March 1984, 236 pp., 350 pta, paperback. Spanish translation. ISBN 84-7574-148-7.

o. As: *Fantasmas* ['Ghosts']. *Tomo 1: Ver Obra Completa* ['Volume I: Complete Works']. __, Spain: Ediciones Forum, S.A., BIBLIOTECA DEL TERROR, March 1984, 144 pp., 175 pta, paperback. Spanish translation. ISBN 84-7574-143-6.

p. As: *Fantasmas* ['Ghosts']. *Tomo 2: Ver Obra Completa* ['Volume 2: Complete Works']. __, Spain: Ediciones Forum, S.A., BIBLIOTECA DEL TERROR, April 1984, 92 pp., 175 pta, paperback. Spanish translation. ISBN 84-7574-144-4.

q. As: *Ghost Story.* New York: Hill House, March 1985, 483 pp., $50.00+s/h, hardcover; boxed, limited edition of 400 copies, signed by Straub and Stephen Gervais (cover artist and illustrator). ISBN 0-931771-00-5.

r. As: *Le Fantôme de Milburn* ['The Phantom of Milburn']. Paris, France: NéO [Nouvelles Éditions Oswald], NÉO PLUS #17, January 1988, 432 pp., 120.00 FF, hardcover. French translation by François Rivière. Illustrated by Jean-Michel Nicollet. ISBN 2-7304-0494-5.

s. As: *Fantasmas* ['Ghosts']. Esplugas de Llobregat (Barcelona, Spain): Plaza & Janés, S. A., March 1989, 504 pp., 1693 pta, paperback. Spanish translation by Lucrecia Moreno de Saenz. ISBN 84-01-32282-0.

t. As: *Het Kwaad.* Utrecht, Netherlands: Uitgeverij Luitingh, 1989, 511 pp., paperback. Dutch translation by Margot Bakker. ISBN 90-245-1665-X.

u. As: *Ghost Story.* Paris, France: Editions Presses Pocket, TERREUR #9033, April 1990, 637 pp., 48.00 FF/7.32 Euro, paperback [*broché*]. French translation by Frank Straschitz. Preface François Rivière. Illustrated by Marc Demoulin. ISBN. 2-266-03481-2.

v. As: *Gengångare* ['Ghost']. Stockholm, Sweden: PAN/Norstedt, 1991, 443 pp., 50:00 SEK (Swedish Kronor), paperback. Swedish translation by Astrid Lundgren. ISBN 9119028512.

w. As: *Ghost Story.* Milano, Italy: Bompiani, 1992, 443 pp., hardcover. Italian translation by Francesco Franconeri. ISBN 88-454-0476-5.

x. As: *Ghost Story.* Denmark: Chr. Erichsen, 1992, 294 pp., paperback. Danish translation by Mogens Kohrt. ISBN 87-555-1255-0.

y. As: *Fantasmas* ['Ghosts']. 3rd edition. Esplugas de Llobregat (Barcelona, Spain): Plaza & Janés, S. A., BIBLIOTECA DE PETER STRAUB #3, April 1993, 560 pp., 869 pta, paperback. Spanish translation by Lucrecia Moreno de Sáenz. ISBN 84-01-49423-0.

z. As: *Ghost Story.* Milano, Italy: Bompiani, 1993, 412 pp., hardcover. Italian translation by Francesco Franconeri.

aa. New York: Pocket Books, October 1994, $6.99, mass-market paperback reissue. ISBN 0-671-68563-5.

bb. As: *Ghost Story.* Milano, Italy: Bompiani, 1994, 443 pp., L14.00 [$6.78], paperback. Italian translation by Francesco Franconeri. ISBN 88-457-2167-9.

cc. As: *Geisterstunde* ['Ghost-Hour']. München, Germany: Wilhelm Heyne Verlag, HEYNE ALLGEMEINE REIHE #09603, 1995, 587 pp., DM 12,90; paperback. German translation by Hanna Molden. ISBN 3-453-08922-7. Reissue, 1998, DM 14.90.

dd. England: Warner, February 1997, 507 pp., £5.99, paperback reprint. ISBN 0-7515-0702-4.

ee. Praha-Plzen, Czech Republic: Beta/Dobrovsky & Secvik, 1997, 462 pp., 269 CZK. Czech translation by Ivo Reitmeyer; cover art by Petr Bauer. ISBN 80-86029-33-6.

ff. As: *Det forfærdligste.* Holland (?): 19__. Dutch translation.

gg. As: *Kuei ti ku shih,* Tai-pei shih: Huang kuan chu poan she, 19__. Chinese translation.

hh. As film: *Ghost Story.* 1981. Universal. Director: John Irvin. Music: Ennio Morricone. Screenplay: Lawrence D. Cohen. Cast: Fred Astaire, Melvyn Douglas, John Houseman, Douglas Fairbanks Jr., Craig Wasson, Patricia Neal, and Alice Krige.

ii. As laser disc. 1981. AV #60274, 1981.

jj. As audiotape: Simon & Schuster Audio, November 1990/January 1991, $15.95, abridged, 2 cassettes, 3 hours. Read by William Windom. ISBN 0-671-72588-2.

SELECTED ARTICLES AND REVIEWS:

1. Adams, Phoebe-Lou. "PLA." *Atlantic Monthly* Vol. 243 (June 1979): 97.
2. Aguirre, Manuel. *The Closed Space: Horror Literature and Western Symbolism.* Manchester and New York: Manchester University Press, 1990. 227. Includes *Ghost Story* in its bibliography of Horror Literature.
3. *Booklist* Vol. 75 (1 June 1979): 1480.
4. *Best Sellers* Vol. 39 (July 1979): 122.
5. Cunningham, Valentine. "Foetality." *New Statesman* Vol. 97 (1 June1979): 796-797. "Invoking and re-enacting the American ghost classic, bringing it up to date, plugging it in to Hollywood's dealings with spooks, *Ghost Story* makes a point about the American imagination" (797).
6. "Damon Knight, Peter Straub, and Iain M. Banks." Online review. 29 July 1998. At: http://www.muohio.edu/~haguecs/ bkrvw/04-27-97.htm. "*Ghost Story* is exactly what it sounds like: it's a ghost story. But in Straub's highly capable hands, the genre is turned inside out. This book has been long recognized as one of the seminal horror works of the last 20 years, and for good reason."
7. Fuller, Edmund. "Spies, Ghosts and Psychological Suspense." *Wall Street Journal* Vol. 193 (2 April 1979): 26.
8. Hill, Douglas. *Maclean's Magazine* Vol. 92 (21 May 1979): 58.
9. Hinckley, Karen, and Barbara Hinckley. "*Ghost Story*." *American Best Sellers: A Reader's Guide to Popular Fiction.* Bloomington and Indianapolis IN: Indianapolis University Press, 1989, hardcover. 105. ISBN 0-253-32728.
10. King, Stephen. *Danse Macabre.* New York: Everest House, July (?) 1981, 400 pp., hardcover. ISBN not given. King's discussion of Ghost Story covers pp. 242-252. Subsequent multiple reprints of *Danse Macabre* in English, French, Italian, Dutch, Spanish, German, and other languages. "Probably *Ghost Story*…is the best of the supernatural novels to be published in the wake of the three books that kicked off a new horror 'wave' in the seventies—those three, of course, being *Rosemary's Baby, The Exorcist*, and *The Other*" [242].
11. *Kirkus Reviews* Vol. 47 (1 February 1979): 152.

12. Koger, Grove. "Genuine Gooseflesh." *Library Journal* Vol. 114 (15 October 1989): 47. Review of paperback edition. "An ambitious and largely successful stab at the Great American Supernatural Novel."

13. Lehmann-Haupt, Christopher. *Books of the Times* [*New York Times*] Vol. 2 (3 April 1979): C11. "If you've a strong predisposition to be frightened by ghost stories, then 'Ghost Story' may well do the trick."

14. *Listener* Vol. 101 (24 May 1979): 724.

15. Lloyd, Valerie. *Newsweek* Vol. 93 (26 March 1979): 104.

16. Lucas, Tim, and Contributing Editors of *Video Times Magazine*. "*Ghost Story.*" *Your Movie Guide to Horror Video Tapes and Discs*. Publications International, 1985. 55-56. Review of film version.

17. Lyons, Gene. "Horror Shocker." *The New York Times Book Review* 8 April 1979: VIII, 14, 23. Critical and partially negative review, concluding, however, that the novel is "a quite sophisticated literary entertainment."

18. Meinert, Renald. "Peter Straub: *Geisterstunde.*" Online review. 4 March 1996. At: http://www.uni-leipzig.de/~braatz/ASFC/SOLARX/SOLARX72/SX72-S55.htm.

19. Neilson, Keith. "Ghost Story." *Horror Literature: A Reader's Guide*. Edited by Neil Barron. New York: Garland, 1990. 303. "*Ghost Story* is one of the seminal works of modern dark fantasy" (304).

20. Neilson, Keith. "*Ghost Story.*" *Survey of Modern Fantasy Literature*. Vol. II. Edited by Frank N. Magill. Englewood Cliffs NJ: Salem Press, 1983: 607-611.

21. *New Statesman & Society* Vol. 3 (7 December 1990): 34.

22. *New York Times Book Review* 25 November 1979: 35. Seasonal advertisement by Coward, McCann & Geoghegan.

23. Nicholls, Peter. "Peter Straub: *Ghost Story.*" *Horror: 100 Best Books*. Edited by Stephen Jones and Kim Newman. Foreword by Ramsey Campbell. New York: Carroll & Graf, 1988, hardcover; 1990, trade paperback. 178-180.

24. *Observer* [London] 27 May 1979: 37.

25. *Publishers Weekly* Vol. 215 (12 February 1979): 113.

26. Ridge, Putney Tyson, Ph.D. (pseudonym for Straub). "Ghost Story." Online: http://net-site.com/straub/ghost.htm.

27. Righton, Barbara. "Snuff the Tragic Dragon." *Maclean's Magazine* Vol. 96, No. 11 (14 March 1983): 50. While the review centers on *Floating Dragon*, Righton includes a number of evaluations of *Ghost Story* as well.

28. Rückbeil, Andrea. "Buchvorstellung: *Geisterstund.*" *Depp* 8 (Germany) 28 May 1988. German-language review of Ghost Story.

At: http://www.snafu.de/~tecumseh/archiv.htm.

29. Skarda, Patricia, and Nora Crow Jaffe, eds. *The Evil Image: Two Centuries of Gothic Short Fiction and Poetry—The Literary Art of Terror from Daniel Defoe to Stephen King*. New York: Meridian/NAL, 1981. 479. Includes the novel in "Suggestions for Further Reading in the Gothic Tradition."

30. Smith, Kristen L. *Library Journal*. Vol. 116 #8 (1 May 1991): 123-124. Review of audio version.

31. Sullivan, Jack. "Night Crawlers." *The Washington Post Book World* 8 April , 1979: L1, L4.

32. *Village Voice Literary Supplement* (May 1993): 25+.

33. *Voice of Youth Advocates* Vol. 6 (December 1983): 267.

34. Wagner, Hank. "A Classic Reconsidered: Peter Straub's *Ghost Story*." *DarkEcho Horror*. March 1999. Online: http://www. dark-echo.com/darkecho/reviews/hankrev.html#classic.

35. Walters, Ray. "Paperback Talk." *New York Times Book Review* Vol. 86 (29 November 1981): 47. The paragraph devoted to *Ghost Story* notes that the film tie-in edition "adds 750,000 copies to the 1,800,000 already sold."

GHOST STORY. London: Jonathan Cape, 1979.

SHADOWLAND. New York: Coward, McCann & Geoghegan, October

A8.

Shadowland (1980)

A8. *SHADOWLAND.* New York: Coward, McCann & Geoghegan, October 1980, 417 pp., $12.95, hardcover, 40,000 copies. ISBN 698-11045-5. Novel.

b. New York: Book-of-the-Month Club, [1980?], hardcover.

c. London: Collins (UK), 1981, 417 pp., £6.95, hardcover. ISBN0-00-222343-0.

d. New York: Berkley Books, 1981, 468 pp., $3.50, mass-market paperback. ISBN 0-425-05056-4.

e. Essex, Great Britain: Fontana/Collins, 1981, 445 pp., 1.75p, mass-market paperback.

f. As: *La Tierra de las Sombras* ['The Land of Shadows']. Buenos Aires, Argentina: Emecé Editores, HISPANIC BOOKS, October 1981, 348 pp., paperback. Spanish translation by Alicia Steimberg. ISBN 9997768094.

g. As: *Schaduwland.* Utrecht, Netherlands: Uitgeverij Luitingh, 1982, 368 pp., paperback. ISBN 90-245-12595-5.

h. As: *Schaduwland.* Utrecht, Netherlands: Veen, Luitingh, 1982, 368 pp., paperback. ISBN 90-204-1201-9.

i. As: *Skuggrike* ['Shadow-Kingdom']. Stockholm, Sweden: Norstedt, 1982, 424 pp., 135:00 SEK (Swedish Kronor), hardcover. Swedish translation by Astrid Lundgren. ISBN 9118223222.

j. As: *La Tierra de las Sombras* ['The Land of Shadows']. Barcelona, Spain: Editorial Bruguera, S.A., BRUGUERA 5 ESTRELLAS #90, January 1983, 544 pp., 900 ptas., paperback. Spanish translation by Alicia Steimberg. ISBN 84-02-09207-1.

k. As: *Schattenland* ['Shadowland']. München, Germany: Wilhelm Heyne Verlag, 1983, 559 pp., DM 9,80; paperback. German translation by Walter Brumm. ISBN 3-453-30937-5.

l. As: *La Tierra de las Sombras* ['The Land of Shadows']. __ : Mundo Actual de Ediciones, S.A., June 1984, 368 pp., 790 ptas., paperback. Spanish translation by Alicia Steimberg. ISBN 84-7475-302-9.

m. As: *La Tierra de las sombras* ['The Land of Shadows']. 2 vols. Vol. 1, Spain: Ediciones Forum, S.A., BIBLIOTECA DEL TERROR, October 1984, 224 pp., 350 pta., paperback. Spanish translation. ISBN 84-7574-230-0. Also issued as: *Tomo 1* [Vol. I]. Ediciones Forum, S.A., BIBLIOTECA DEL TERROR, October 1984, 120 pp., 175 pta, paperback. Spanish translation. ISBN 84-7574-228-9. *Tomo II* [Vol. 2.] Spain: Ediciones Forum, S.A., BIBLIOTECA DEL TERROR, October 1984, 124 pp., paperback. Spanish translation. ISBN 84-7574-229-7.

n. New York: Berkeley, November 1985, 468 pp., $4.50, mass-market paperback reissue. ISBN 0-425-08207-5. 13th printing by 1999.

o. New York: Berkeley, 1987, $6.99, mass-market paper. ISBN 0-425-09726-9.

p. As: *Shadowland.* Paris, France: J'ai Lu, ÉPOUVANTE #2249, August 1987, 508 pp., 47.00 FF, paperback. French translation by Jean-Paul Martin. Illustrated by Franco Accornero. ISBN 2-277-22249-6.

q. London: Fontana, September 1989, 478 pp., £3.99, mass-market paperback. ISBN 0-00-616546-X. 7th printing.

r. As: *Skuggrike* ['Shadow-Kingdom']. Stockholm, Sweden: PAN Norstedt, 1992, 424 pp., 50:00 SEK (Swedish Kronor), paperback. Swedish translation by Astrid Lundgren. ISBN 911902861X.

s. London: Grafton, June 1993, 478 pp., £4.99, paperback. Cover art by Melvyn Grant. ISBN 0-00-616546-X.

t. As: *Kraina Ceieni.* Poznan, Poland: Dom Wydawniczy Rebis, 1993, 420 pp., 69.000zl, paperback. Polish translation by Irena Lipinska. ISBN 83-85696-65-2.

u. New York: Berkeley, November 1994, $7.50, mass-market paperback reissue. ISBN 0425097269.

v. Springfield PA: Gauntlet Publications, August 1995, 598 pp., $60.00+s/h, slipcased limited edition; signed by Straub, Ramsey Campbell, and Thomas Tessier, 500 copies. Includes cover art by Harry O. Morris; flap copy by 'Putney Tyson Ridge' (pseudonym for Straub); Preface by Peter Straub; Foreword by Ramsey Campbell; Afterword by Thomas Tessier. ISBN 1-887368-00-0.

w. As: *Shadowland.* Paris, France: J'ai Lu, ÉPOUVANTE ['Horror' collection], December 1996, 47.00 FF/7.17 Euro, paperback [*broché*]. French translation. ISBN 2290022497.

   x. As: *Schattenland*. Augsburg, Germany [Bavaria]: Bechtermunz Verlag, 1996, 559 pp., hardcover. ISBN 3-86047-522-3.

   y. Paris: Livres de Poches, 19__, paperback. French translation.

   z. As screenplay adaptation: *King of the Cats*, by Greg Addison Hill, Jr. Darkmoor Studios and Arkham Graphics. Reference at: http://www.darkmoor.com/crypt/kingcats.htm.

COMMENTS: The novel was nominated for the World Fantasy Award, 1981. The first of Straub's novels for which advance uncorrected proofs included cover art.

SELECTED ARTICLES AND REVIEWS:

1. *Best Sellers* Vol. 40 (December 1980): 315.
2. *Business Week* 22 December 1980: 9.
3. Hemesath, James E. *Library Journal* Vol. 105 (15 October 1980): 2235. "...[A]n ambitious patchwork fantasy of shifting reality."
4. *Kirkus Reviews* Vol. 48 (1 September 1980): 1187.
5. Kliatt Young Adult Paperback Book Guide Vol. 16 (Winter 1982): 17.
6. Lehmann-Haupt, Christopher. *The New York Times* 24 October 1980: III, 31.
7. *The Listener* Vol. 105 (16 April 1981): 517.
8. Matthews, Barbara. "Much Less Here than Meets the Eye." *Maclean's Magazine* Vol. 94, No. 1 (12 January 1981): 44.
9. Nathan, Paul. "Delvers and Disablers." *Publishers Weekly* Vol. 242, No. 15 (10 April 1995): 17. Brief article on the sale of option rights for *Shadowland*.
10. Neilson, Keith. "Shadowland." *Horror Literature: A Reader's Guide*. Edited by Neil Barron. New York: Garland, 1990. 304.
11. *New Statesman* Vol. 101 (17 April 1981): 20.
12. *Publishers Weekly* Vol. 218 (19 September 1980): 144.
13. *Publishers Weekly* Vol. 220 (25 September 1981): 87.
14. Ridge, Putney Tyson, Ph.D. (pseudonym for Straub). "*Shadowland*: Thoughts of an Intimate Friend." Online: http://netsite.com/straub/put_sha.htm.
15. Suttcliffe, Thomas. "Getting the Wind Up." *The Times Literary Supplement* No. 4072 (17 April 1981): 430.
16. *School Library Journal* Vol. 27 (February 1981): 82.
17. *Voice of Youth Advocates* Vol. 4 (February 1982): 38.
18. Village Voices Literary Supplement (May 1993): 25+.
19. *Wilson Library Bulletin* Vol. 55 (April 1981): 615.

SHADOWLAND

Peter Straub

SHADOWLAND. Springfield PA: Gauntlet Publications, August 1995

FLOATING DRAGON. New York: G. P. Putnam's, February 1983.

A9.
Floating Dragon
(1982)

A9. *FLOATING DRAGON*. San Francisco CA, Columbia PA: Underwood-Miller, November 1982, 560 pp., $50.00, hardcover, numbered edition of 500 copies, signed by Straub and Leo and Diane Dillon (jacket designers). ISBN 0-934438-68-4. Novel.

b. New York: G. P. Putnam's, February 1983. 515 pp., $15.95, hardcover, 40,000 copies. ISBN 0-399-12772-0.

c. London: Collins, 1983, 623 pp., £9.95, hardcover. Cover art by Terry Oakes. First British Edition. ISBN 0-00-222714-2.

d. As: *Dragón* ['Dragon']. Esplugas de Llobregat (Barcelona, Spain): Plaza & Janés Editores, GRAN PARADA, May 1983, 448 pp., 825 pta [$9.50], trade paperback. Spanish translation by J. Ferrer Aleu. ISBN 84-01-36040-4.

e. New York: G. P. Putnam's Sons, September 1983, 544 pp., hardcover. No ISBN listed. Book Club Edition.

f. As: *El Dragón flotante* ['The Floating Dragon']. Panama: Printer Internacional de Panamá, January 1984, 616 pp., hardcover. Spanish translation by J. Ferrar Aleu. ISBN 84-8386-326-X.

g. New York: Berkeley, March 1984, 595 pp., $3.95, paperback reprint. ISBN 0-425-06285-6.

h. As: *Drakens Dag* ['Dragon's Day']. Stockholm, Sweden: Norstedt, 1984, 575 pp., 160:00 SEK (Swedish Kronor), hardcover. Swedish translation by Astrid Lundgren. ISBN 9118421024.

i. As: *Draakengif* ['Dragon-Poison']. Utrecht, Netherlands: L. J. Veen, B. J., 1984, 438 pp., trade paperback. Dutch translation by Margot Bakker. ISBN 90-204-3786-0.

j. New York: Berkeley, November 1985, 595 pp., $4.95, paperback reprint. ISBN 0-425-08206-7.

MICHAEL R. COLLINGS

k. London: Fontana, April 1986, 623 pp., £2.95, paperback. ISBN 0-00-616494-3. Reissued 1989, £4.50; 1991, £4.99.

l. New York: Berkeley, 1987, 608 pp., $6.99, mass-market paper. ISBN 0-425-09725-0.

m. As: *Dragon flottant* ['Floating Dragon']. Paris, France: J'ai Lu, ÉPOUVANTE #2373, April 1988, 502 pp., 47.00 FF, paperback. French translation by Jean-Paul Martin. Illustrated by Matthieu Blanchin. ISBN 2-277-22373-5.

n. As: *Drago del male* ['Dragon of Evil']. Milano, Italy: Sperling and Kupfer, [1989?], 502 pp., 21.900 L, hardcover. Italian translation by Tullio Dobner. ISBN 88-200-0538-7.

o. As: *Drago del male* ['Dragon of Evil']. Milano, Italy: Sperling Paperback, SUPER BESTSELLER, 1990, 502 pp., 15.000 L [$7.26], paperback. Italian translation by Tullio Dobner.

p. As: *Dragón* ['Dragon']. Esplugas de Llobregat (Barcelona, Spain): Plaza & Janés Editores, GRAN PARADA, May 1983, 448 pp., 825 pta, paperback. Spanish translation by J. Ferrer Aleu. ISBN 84-01-49091-X. Also issued as: *Dragón*. Esplugas de Llobregat (Barcelona, Spain): Plaza & Janés Editores, GRAN PARADA, May 1983, 448 pp., $9.50, trade paperback. Spanish translation by J. Ferrer Aleu. ISBN 84-01-36040-4.

q. As: *Drakens Dag* ['Dragon's Day']. Stockholm, Sweden: PAN/Norstedt, 1991, 575 pp., 50:00 SEK (Swedish Kronor), paperback. Swedish translation by Astrid Lundgren. ISBN 9119028717.

r. London: Grafton, June 1993, 655 pp., £5.99, paperback reissue. ISBN 0-00-616494-3. Cover art by Melvyn Grant.

s. New York: Berkeley, November 1994, __ pp., $7.99, mass-market reissue paperback edition. ISBN 0425097250.

t. As: *Lohikäärme* ['Dragon']. Finland: Book Studio Oy, 1995. Finnish translation by Pertti Koskela.

u. As: *Der Hauch des Drachen* ['The Breath of the Dragon']. München, Germany: Wilhelm Heyne Verlag, HEYNE ALLGEMEINE REIHE #09751, 1996, 732 pp., DM 16,90; Paperback. ISBN 3-453-09274-0

v. As: *Dragon flottant* ['Floating Dragon']. Paris, France: J'ai Lu, BARBARA CARTLAND COLLECTION, June 1997, 47.00 FF/7.17 Euro. French translation. ISBN 2290057495.

w. As: *Dragon flottant* ['Floating Dragon']. Paris, France: J'ai Lu, ÉPOUVANTE ['Horror' collection], June 1997, 47.00 FF/7.17 Euro. French translation. ISBN 2290023736.

    x. As: *Dragon flottant* ['Floating Dragon']. Paris, France: Livres de Poches, 19__, paperback. French translation .

    y. As audiotape: Listen for Pleasure, Inc., January 1987, abridged, 2 cassettes. Read by Fritz Weaver. ISBN 0886461995.

COMMENTS: Received the British Fantasy Award, Best Novel, 1983 and the August Derleth Award. There have been at least five reprints of the hardcover edition.

SELECTED ARTICLES AND REVIEWS:

1. *Books & Bookmen* (February 1983): 32.
2. *Books & Bookmen* (January 1984): 37.
3. *Booklist* Vol. 79 (1 October 1982): 45.
4. *Best Sellers* Vol. 43 (April 1983): 10.
5. Collins, Robert A. Review. *Fantasy Newsletter* No. 57 (March 1983).
6. Collins, Robert A. Review. *Science Fiction & Fantasy Book Review.* Issue 4 (May 1983):46-47. "...[I]t's a horror novel, loaded with gore—tides, streams, lakes and rivers of it."
7. Dorey, Alan. *Paperback Inferno* #47, Volume 7, No 5, 43rd issue (April 1984).
8. Freedman, Richard. *New York Times Book Review* Vol. 88 (6 March 1983): VIII, 10.
9. Hemesath, James E. *Library Journal* Vol. 107 (1 November 1982): 2110. " "This very ambitious novel features a baker's dozen of well-developed characters and a multitude of scary scenes. Nevertheless, it might well be too long and too complicated for its own good."
10. *Kirkus Review* Vol. 50 (15 November 1982): 1261.
11. Lehmann-Haupt, Christopher. "Floating Dragon." *The New York Times* Vol. 132 (20 January 1983): III, 22:3. "I'm not certain whether it's simply the believable premise he's set up or it's because experience has given him a firmer command of his effects, but I was fairly awed by some of the more nightmarish scenes in 'Floating Dragon.'"
12. Lochte, Dick. "Book Notes: Author, Author." *Los Angeles Times Book Review* 30 January 1983: 6. One-sentence notice of *Floating Dragon.*
13. *Magazine of Fantasy and Science Fiction* Vol. 64 (June 1983): 27.
14. Neilson, Keith. "Floating Dragon." *Horror Literature: A Reader's Guide.* Edited by Neil Barron. New York: Garland, 1990. 303.
15. *New Statesman* Vol. 105 (25 February 1983): 28.
16. *New York Times Book Review* Vol. 89 (26 February 1984): 38. Brief review in "New & Noteworthy" section.
17. *The Observer* [London] 20 February 1983: 33.

18. *Publishers Weekly* Vol. 222 (12 November 1982): 59.
19. *Publishers Weekly* Vol. 225 (10 February 1984): 193.
20. *Quill & Quire* [Canada] Vol. 49 (May 1983): 36.
21. Ridge, Putney Tyson, Ph.D. (pseudonym for Straub). "*Floating Dragon.*" Online: http://net-site.com/straub/pt_drag.htm.
22. Righton, Barbara. "Snuff the Tragic Dragon." *Maclean's Magazine* Vol. 96, No. 11 (March 14, 1983): 50.
23. Ryan, Alan. "What Evil Lurks in the Heart of Hampstead?" *Washington Post Book World* Vol. 13 (13 February 1983): 3, 6. "Straub is a deliberately literary writer, conscious of and unembarrassed by his debt to both antecedents and contemporaries....If *Floating Dragon* is sometimes baffling, flawed in some structural elements, and perhaps a little too long for its own good, it is at the same time both ruthlessly contemporary and steeped in tradition, gruesomely chilling, and told with a narrative strength and lively colloquial style that readers should welcome" (6).
24. Schlobin, Roger. "Second Opinion." *Science Fiction & Fantasy Review* Issue 14 (May 1983): 48. "It is the majestic triumph of the four protagonists—one female, one young, one old, one middleaged—that, in part distinguishes *Floating Dragon* from more pedestrian examples of the genre. In most horror fiction, release from terror is the characters' greatest hope. However, in *Floating Dragon*, there is a sense of epic triumph as well as relief."
25. *Science Fiction Chronicle* Vol. 8 (July 1987): 50. Review of audio version.
26. *Science Fiction Review* Vol. 13 (August 1984): 28.
27. *Village Voice Literary Supplement* (May 1993): 25+.
28. *West Coast Review of Books* Vol. 9 (March 1983): 39.

FLOATING DRAGON. San Francisco CA, Columbia PA: Underwood-Miller,
November 1982.

A10.

The General's Wife

(1982)

A10. *THE GENERAL'S WIFE*. West Kingston RI: Donald M. Grant, November 1982, 128 pp., $__, hardcover, signed and numbered, 1200 copies. Illustrated by Tom Canty; Introduction by Straub. ISBN 0937986542. [See also B1]

COMMENTS: See also under "Short Fiction" for original magazine appearance of this novella. Donald M. Grants notes that the edition has been sold out for many years [2/99].

SELECTED ARTICLES AND REVIEWS:
1. Breque, Jean-Daniel. Review. *Science Fiction & Fantasy Newsletter* Issue 18 (October 1983): 36-37. "This haunting, enigmatic story is somewhat reminiscent of Henry James....As an *objet d'art*, the book is nothing short of stunning. Exquisite *fin de siecle* design and sub-dued pencil drawings by Thomas Canty, very fine binding...."

LEESON PARK AND BELSIZE SQUARE: POEMS 1970-1975. San Francisco CA, Columbia PA: Underwood-Miller, October 1983.

A11.

Leeson Park and Belsize Square

(1983)

A11. *LEESON PARK AND BELSIZE SQUARE: POEMS 1970-1975.* San Francisco CA, Columbia PA: Underwood-Miller, October 1983, 74 pp., hardcover. limited, signed, numbered edition, $30.00, 200 copies. ISBN 0-934438-90-0. Poetry.

    b. San Francisco CA, Columbia PA: Underwood-Miller, October 1983, 74 pp. hardcover; presentation edition of 20 copies. ISBN 0-934438-90-0.

    c. San Francisco CA, Columbia PA: Underwood-Miller, October 1983, 74 pp., $9.95, hardcover; trade edition of 780 copies. ISBN 0-934438-91-9.

CONTENTS. I: "Facing the Lavish Weather" [see D43]; "Facing Land's End" [see D44]; "The Figures on the Beach" [see D46]; "Reading the Well" [see D47]; "My Life in Pictures" [see D1]; "Encantadas" [see D41];

    II ISHMAEL: "The First Bedouin" [see A2, D7]; "The Desert Motion" [see A2, D]; "Ishmael's Song to His Sister" [see A2, D8]; "The Bow" [see A2, D3]; "Using the Bow" [see A2, D4]; "Ishmael in Manhattan" [see A2, D9]; "Downtown, Way Down" [see A2, D10]; "The Music He Hears" [see A2, D11]; "The Sleepers" [see A2, D5]; "Song for One on Water" [see A2, D12]; "A Loosening, A Spending Prose" [see A2, D13]; "From Lawrence's Letters" [see A2, D14]; "On Hampstead Heath with Women" [see A2, D6]; "*Envoi From A Brother*" [see A2, D15];

    III: "A Triple-Decker Novel" [see D45]; "For Ann Lauterbach" [see D48]; "From the Heian Court" [see D49]; "Coming to Rest" [see D50]; "Photographic Plate" [see D51]; "Withstanding, Saving,

Moving" [see D52]; "Making the Circle's Figure: Five French Poems" [see D42]; "Lichens" [see D53]; "The Trace: I Buried Day; II Trace" [see D54];

IV: "Lessive" [see D55]; "Sentences for Rimbaud" [see D56]; "For Thomas Tessier" [see D57]; "Text" [see D58]

SELECTED ARTICLES AND REVIEWS:

1. Neilson, Keith. "Academic Poetry." *Fantasy Review* Vol. 7, #70 (August 1984): 27-28. "With this collection of poems Peter Straub consolidates his reputation as the most literary of contemporary horror fiction authors."
2. *Publishers Weekly* Vol. 224 (4 November 1983): 56.
3. Ridge, Putney Tyson, Ph.D. (pseudonym for Straub). "*Leeson* Park and Belsize Square." Online: http://net-site.com/straub/pt _lees.htm.

THE TALISMAN, with Stephen King. New York: Viking/G. P. Putnam's Sons, 8 November 1984.

A12.

The Talisman (1984)

A12. *THE TALISMAN*, with Stephen King. New York: Viking/G. P. Putnam's Sons, 8 November 1984, x+646 pp., $18.95, hardcover, 500,000 copies. ISBN 0-670-69199-2. Novel.

    b. West Kingston RI: Donald M. Grant, 1984, 2 volumes; hardcover, limited slipcased edition, 70 presentation copies; signed by Stephen King, Straub, and the illustrators. Signature page reads: "This presentation copy #[ ] of 70 copies of this special illustrated first edition of The Talisman is signed by the participants in this edition and is not for sale."

    c. London: Viking/Penguin U.K., October 1984, 646 pp., £9.95, hardcover. Appeared simultaneously with the American edition although scheduled to appear earlier.

    d. As: *El Talisman*. Barcelona, Spain: Editorial Planeta, S.A., 1984. Spanish translation.

    e. West Kingston RI: Donald M. Grant, February 1985, 2 vols., 464 pp.+336 pp., $120.00, hardcover; signed, numbered, limited, slipcased edition, 1200 copies. Ten full-color illustrations. ISBN 0-937986-65-8.

    f. West Kingston RI: Donald M. Grant, February 1985, 464 pp.+336 pp., $65.00, hardcover; slipcased trade edition. ISBN 0-937986-66-6.

    g. London: Penguin Books, August 1985, 784 p., paperback.

    h. New York: Berkeley, November 1985, 770 pp., $4.95, mass-market paperback. ISBN 0-42-08181-8.

    i. As: *De Talisman*. Utrecht, Netherlands: Uitgeverji, L. J. Veen, B. J., 1985, 470 p., trade paperback. Dutch translation by Margot Bakker; abridged (approximately 100 pages deleted). ISBN. 90-204-08-615. 3rd printing, 1986. Also as: ISBN 90-245-26-965.

    j. As: *The Talisman*. __: Israel, 1985, 606 pp., hardcover.

    k. As: *Mo Fu*. Ta-pei shih: Huang kuan chu pan she, 1985, 495 pp. Chinese translation.

l. As: *Der Talisman*. Hamburg, West Germany: Hoffman & Campe Verlag, 1986, 716 p., hardcover. German translation by Christel Wiemken. ISBN 3-455-03737-2.

m. As: *Il Talismano*. Milano, Italy: Sperling & Kupfer, 1986, 655 pp., paperback. Italian translation by Tullio Dobner.

n. As: *Le Talisman*. Paris, France: Editions Albin Michel #7075, 1986, 1084 pp., paperback. French translation by Beatrice Gartenberg and Isabelle Delord. ISBN 88-200-0522-0.

o. As: *Le Talisman des Territoires* ['The Talisman of the Territories']. Paris, France: Éditions Robert Laffont, BEST SELLERS, APRIL 1986, 649 pp., 120.00 FF, hardcover. French translation by Béatrice Gartenberg and Isabelle Delord. ISBN 2-221-04819-9.

p. As: *Talismanen*. Stockholm, Sweden: Legenda, 1986, 798 pp., 202:00 SEK (Swedish Kronor), hardcover. Swedish translation by Lennart Olofsson. ISBN 9158207155.

q. As: *Le Talisman*. Paris, France: Livre de Poche [LGF] Science-Fiction #7075, April 1987, 1085 pp., 48.00 FF, paperback. French translation by Béatrice Gartenberg and Isabelle Delord. ISBN 2-253-04181-5.

r. As: *Der Talisman*. Stuttgart, Germany: Deutscher Bücherbund, 1987. German translation by Cristel Wiemken.

s. As: *Der Talisman*. Götersloh, Austria: Bertelsmann Lesering, 1987. German translation by Cristel Wiemken.

t. As: *Talismanen*. Stockholm: Legenda/Norstedt, 1987, 798 pp., 112:00 SEK (Swedish Kronor), hardcover without dust jacket. Swedish translation by Lennart Olaffson. ISBN 1958211357.

u. As: *Talismanen*. Stockholm: Legenda/Norstedt, 1987, 798 pp., 56:50 SEK (Swedish Kronor), paperback. Swedish translation by Lennart Olaffson. ISBN 9158212442.

v. As: *Talismanen*. Höganäs, Sweden: Bro Böcker, 1987, 798 pp. Book Club Edition. Swedish translation by Lennart Olofsson.

w. As: *The Talisman*. 2 volumes. Tokyo, Japan: Kozaburo Yano, 1987, 578 pp. (Vol. I), 566 pp. (Vol.2), 1280 Y, paperback. ISBN 4-10-219308-1 (Vol. 1); 4-10-219309-X (Vol. 2).

x. As: *Der Talisman*. München: Wilhelm Heyne Verlag, HEYNE ALLGEMEINE REIHE TB-07662, 1988, DM 16,90, hardcover. German translation by Cristel Wiemken. ISBN 3-453-02523-7.

y. As: *Talismano*. Milano, Italy: Sperling Paperback, 1988, 655 pp., L 15.000, paperback. Italian translation.

z. New York: Berkeley, January 1991, $7.99, mass-market paperback reissue. ISBN 0425105334.

aa. As: *Talismaani*. Hyvinkaa, Finland: Hangon Kirjapaino Oy, 1991, 859 pp., paperback. Finnish translation by Kari Salminen. ISBN 951-611-418-0 (sid), 951-611-427-X (nid).

bb. As: *El talismán*. Barcelona, Spain: Editorial Planeta S.A., August 1992, 569 pp., 962 pta, paperback. Spanish translation by Pilar Giralt Gorina. ISBN 84-08-00073-X.

cc. As *Talismanen*. Stockholm, Sweden: Natur & Kultur/Norstedts, 1994, 798 pp., 77:00 SEK (Swedish Kronor), paperback. Swedish translation by Lennart Olofsson. ISBN 9127051838.

dd. As: *Talizman*. Budapest, Hungary: Europa Konyukiado, 1994, 857 pp., 598 ft, paperback. Hungarian translation by Zentai Eva. ISBN 963-07-5752-4.

ee. As: *Talizman*. Warszawa, Poland: Wydawnictwo Amber, 1994, 376 pp., paperback. Polish translation by Anna Kidawa and Sylwia Twardo. ISBN 83-7082-292-4.

ff. As: *El talismán*. __: RBA Coleccionables, January 1995, 576 pp., 966 pta, trade paperback. Spanish translation by Pilar Giralt Gorina. ISBN 84-473-0727-1.

gg. As: *Der Talisman*. München, Germany: Wilhelm Heyne Verlag, 1995, 714 pp., DM 16,90; paperback. German translation by Christel Wiemken. ISBN 3-453-02523-7.

hh. As: *Il Talismano*. 2nd edition. Bologna, Italy: Sperling & Kupfer, March 1996, 664 pp., L 32.900 [$15.92]. Italian translation.

ii. London: New English Library, July 1996, 768 pp., £6.99, paperback. Cover art by Steve Crisp. ISBN 0-340-67445-8.

jj. Czech Republic: Perseus, 1996, 638 pp., 279 CZK. Czech translation by Ivo Reitmayer; cover art by Petr Bauer.

kk. As: *Le Talisman des Territoires* ['The Talisman of the Territories']. Paris, France: Éditions Robert Laffont, BEST SELLERS, June 1996, 654 pp., 149.00FF/ 22.71 Euro, trade paperback. French translation by Béatrice Gartenberg and Isabelle Delord. ISBN 2221086058.

ll. As: *Le Talisman*. Paris, France: Le Livre de Poche, 1997, 920 pp., paperback. Illustrated by Philippe Bouchet. French translation by Béatrice Gartenberg and Isabelle Delord. ISBN 2-253-04181-5.

mm. As: *The Talisman*. Russia, 1997, 685 pp., hardcover. Russian translation by A. A. Kydpreuya. ISBN 5-15-000239-9.

nn. As: *El talismán*. Barcelona, Spain: Editorial Planeta S.A., February 1998, 576 pp., 1298 pta, paperback.. Spanish translation by Pilar Giralt Gorina. ISBN 84-08-02430-2.

oo. Film rights: Steven Spielberg and Amblin Entertainment. Screen adaptation: Richard Lagravenese (May 22 1992). Film unproduced as of 1999.

pp. No audiotape adaptation

COMMENTS: The novel was nominated for the World Fantasy Award, 1985.

SELECTED ARTICLES AND REVIEWS:
1. Adler, Constance. "Prince of Darkness: In His Reign of Best-selling Terror, Author Stephen King Remains Absolute Master of the Scary Story." *Philadelphia Magazine* 76 (August 1985): 85+. [3-page article]
2. Amantia, A. M. B. *Library Journal* 109 (November 1, 1984): 2080.
3. Anders, Smiley. "Blockbuster of a Fantasy Tale Gets Guidance from Twain." In *Morning Advocate* [Baton Rouge, LA] (November 18, 1984). As microfiche: *NewsBank*: Literature 11 (December, 1984): Fiche 58, A8-A9.
4. Beagle, Peter. "King Plus Straub Equals Pure Cliché." *San Jose Mercury News* [California] 28 October, 1984. As microfiche: *NewsBank*: Literature 11 (November 1984): Fiche 45, G14-46, A1.
5. Beahm, George. *The Stephen King Companion*. Kansas City, MO: Andrews and McMeel, September 1989, 365 pp., $10.95, trade paperback. 280-283. ISBN 0-8362-7978-6. Multiple reissues. Article.
6. Blue, Tyson. "Collaboration of Two Masterful Authors Produces a Suspenseful 'The Talisman.'" *Courier Herald* [Dublin, GA] 10 November, 1984.
7. Blue, Tyson. "Talisman Limited Review." *Castle Rock: The Stephen King Newsletter* 3:1 (December 1986-January 1987): 6.
8. *Booklist* 81 (January 15, 1985): 686.
9. Bosky, Bernadette. "Stephen King and Peter Straub: Fear and Friendship." *Discovering Stephen King*. Edited by Darrell Schweitzer. STARMONT STUDIES IN LITERARY CRITICISM #8. Mercer Island, WA: Starmont House, 1985. 55-82.
10. Cheuse, Alan. "A Sci-Fi Quest Novel from King and Straub." *Los Angeles Herald Examiner* 18 November 1984. As microfiche:

NewsBank: Literature 11 (December, 1984): Fiche 57, G12-G14.

11. Clark, Theresa J. *Saturday Review* (November/December 1984): 85.

12. Collings, Michael R. *The Annotated Guide to Stephen King: A Primary and Secondary Bibliography of the Works of America's Premier Horror Writer* Mercer Island, WA: Starmont House, STARMONT REFERENCE GUIDE #8, October 1986, 176 pp., $17.95, hardcover. 17-18. ISBN 0-930261-81-X. Issued simultaneously as paperback, $9.95. ISBN 0-930261-80-1. ISSN 0738-0127.

13. ———. *The Many Facets of Stephen King.* Mercer Island, WA: Starmont House, STARMONT STUDIES IN LITERARY CRITICISM #11, 1986, 190 pp., $17.95, hardcover. 126-138. ISBN 0-930261-15-1. Issued simultaneously as paperback, $9.95. ISBN 0-930261-14-3. ISSN 0737-1306.

14. ———. *The Stephen King Phenomenon.* Mercer Island, WA: Starmont House, STARMONT STUDIES IN LITERARY CRITICISM #14, 1987, 144 pp., $17.95, hardcover. 55-57, 84-90. ISBN 0-930261-13-5. Issued simultaneously as paperback, $9.95. ISBN 0-930261-12-7. ISSN 0737-1306.

15. ———. *The Work of Stephen King: An Annotated Bibliography and Guide.* Series Editor: Boden Clarke. San Bernardino CA: Borgo Press, BIBLIOGRAPHIES OF MODERN AUTHORS #25, 1996, 480 pp., $41.00, hardcover. 80-85. ISBN 0-8095-1520-7. Issued simultaneously as paperback, $31.00. ISBN 0-8095-1520-2. ISSN 0749-470X.

16. ———. *Scaring Us to death: The Impact of Stephen King on Popular Culture.* 2nd edition, revised and expanded. San Bernardino CA: Borgo Press, MILFORD SERIES: POPULAR WRITERS OF TODAY #63, 1997, 168 pp., $31.00, hardcover. Esp. 52-53, 63-65, 130-132. ISBN 0-930261-37-2. Issued simultaneously in paperback, $21.00. ISBN 0-930261-38-0. ISSN 0163-2469.

17. Cortland, Will. "The King of Bump in the Night." *Dodge Adventurer* (Spring, 1985): 17-18. As: "The Adventurer Looks at Stephen King." *Castle Rock: The Stephen King Newsletter* 1:6 (June, 1985): 11.

18. D'Angelo, John. "'Talisman' Tells of Modern-Day Huckleberry Finn." *Pittsburgh Press* 2 December 1984. As microfiche: *NewsBank*: Literature 11 (December, 1984): Fiche 58, A14.

19. Eaglen, Audrey. *Voice of Youth Advocates* (April 1985): 49.

20. *English Journal* 74 (December, 1985): 57.

21. *Esquire* 102 (November, 1984): 231.

22. Fazell, Daryl. "King and Straub Weave a Snug Yarn," *St. Petersburg Times* [Florida] 28 October 1984. As microfiche: *NewsBank*: Literature 11 (November, 1984): Fiche 46, A2.

23. Goldstein, William. "A Coupl'a Authors Sittin' Around Talkin'." *Publishers Weekly* (May, 11, 1984). Rpt. in *The Stephen King Companion*. Edited by George Beahm. Kansas City, MO: Andrews and McMeel, September 1989, paper, p. 283-287. Graham, Mark. "Masters of the Macabre." *Rocky Mountain News* [Denver CO] 7 October 1984: 34M.

24. Grooms, Roger. "'Talisman' Not Without Macabre Charm." *Cincinnati Enquirer* [OH] 21 October 1984. As microfiche: *NewsBank*: Literature 11 (November, 1984): Fiche 46, A10.

25. Harvey, L. J. "Unlucky 'Talisman' Defeats Horror King." *Kansas City Star* [MO] 4 November 1984). As microfiche: *NewsBank*: Literature 11 (November, 1984): Fiche 46, A5.

26. Herbert, Frank. "When Parallel Worlds Collide." *Washington Post Book World* 14 (October 14, 1984): 1-2.

27. Herron, Don, ed. *Reign of Fear*. Los Angeles: Underwood-Miller, June 1988, 254 pp., $75.00, hardcover. ISBN 0-88733-061-4.

28. Kernan, Michael. "Kindred Spirits: Horror Pros Stephen King and Peter Straub Put Their Skills Together for a Best Seller." *Washington Post* 107 , 27 November 1984: C1.

29. "King Rejects Book Club Offer for *The Talisman*." *Science Fiction Chronicle* 6:4 (January, 1985): 4.

30. Kirk, Robin. "King and Straub, Masters of Horror, Team Up for Highly Derivative Yawner." *Tribune* [Oakland CA] 18 November 1984. As microfiche: *NewsBank*: Literature 11 (December 1984): Fiche 58, A1.

31. *Kirkus Reviews* 52 (August 15, 1984): 771.

32. *Kliatt Young Adult Paperback Book Guide* 20 (Spring 1986): 22.

33. Leerhsen, Charles. "The Titans of Terror." *Newsweek* (December 24, 1984): 61-62.

34. Lehmann-Haupt, Christopher. *New York Times Daily* 8 November 1984: III, 27.

35. Lewis, Don. "'Talisman' Good, But No Supernovel." *Milwaukee Journal* [WI] 11 November 1984. As microfiche: *NewsBank*: Literature 11 (December 1984): Fiche 58, B4.

36. Liberatore, Karen. "Jack Sawyer in Fantasyland." *San Francisco Examiner* 7 October 1984. As microfiche: *NewsBank*: Literature 11 (November 1984): Fiche 45, G12-G13.

37. Lileks, James. "A Horror Novel That's a Splatter Version of 'The Wizard of Oz.'" *Minnesota Star and Tribune* 25 November 1984. As microfiche: *NewsBank*: Literature 11 (December 1984): Fiche 58, A10.

38. *The Magazine of Fantasy & Science Fiction* 68 (March, 1985): 16.

39. Magistrale, Tony. *Landscape of Fear: Stephen King's American Gothic.* Bowling Green, OH: Bowling Green State University Popular Press, March 1988, trade paperback.

40. ———. *The Moral Voyages of Stephen King.* Mercer Island, WA: Starmont House, STARMONT STUDIES IN LITERARY CRITICISM #25, 1989, hardcover. Issued simultaneously in paperback.

41. McC.Dresser, Sheila. "One Good Book by Two Masters of the Best-Seller List." *Sun* [Baltimore MD] 4 November 1984. As microfiche: *NewsBank*: Literature 11 (November, 1984): Fiche 46, A3.

42. McLaurin, Preston. "Epic Tale from Masters of Macabre." *State* [Columbia SC] 11 November 1984. As microfiche: *NewsBank*: Literature 11 (December, 1984): Fiche 58, B1.

43. Merritt, Robert. "Horrors! King, Straub Turn to Fantasy." *Richmond Times-Dispatch* [VA] 28 October 1984. As microfiche: *NewsBank*: Literature 11 (November 1984): Fiche 46, A11.

44. Miller, Faren. "*The Talisman:* Stephen King & Peter Straub." *Locus* 17:10, No. 285 (October 1984). Review.

45. Millhiser, Marlys. "When Nit Comes to Grit." *Denver Post* [CO] 18 November 1984. As microfiche: *NewsBank*: Literature 11 (December 1984): Fiche 58, A3.

46. Nathan, Paul S. "The Talisman and the Clubs." *Publishers Weekly* (November 23, 1984): 28.

47. Perry, Pamela M. "Lack of Structure Main Weakness of 'Talisman.'" *Atlanta Journal-Constitution* [GA] 4 November 1984. As microfiche: *NewsBank*: Literature 11 (December 1984): Fiche 58, A6.

48. Pollack, Dale. "Fantasy Quest for the Reel Thing." *Los Angeles Times Book Review* (November 18, 1984): 13.

49. *Publishers Weekly* 228 (September 20, 1985): 107.

50. Reino, Joseph. *Stephen King: The First Decade, Carrie to Pet Sematary.* Twayne's United States Authors Series (TUSAS 531). Edited by Warren French. Boston: Twayne Publishers, February 1988.

51. Reuter, Madalynne. "502,000 Copies of *Talisman* Shipped in One Day." *Publishers Weekly* (October 26, 1984): 25.

52. Richmond, Peter. "Striking Out With King (and Straub)." *Miami Herald* [FL] 25 November 1984. As microfiche: *NewsBank*: Literature 11 (December 1984): Fiche 58, A4-A5.

53. Rothenstein, Richard. "Two Terror Titans Team Up." *Daily News* [NY] 14 October 1984. As microfiche: *NewsBank*: Literature 11 (November 1984): Fiche 45, G10-G11.

54. Saidman, Anne. *Stephen King: Master of Horror.* Minneapolis MN: Lerner Publications Company, THE ACHIEVERS, 1992, 56 pp., library-binding hardcover. 39-41. ISBN 0-8225-0545-2. Also issued in paperback, ISBN 0-8225-9623-7. Overview of *The Talisman* written for juvenile readers.

55. Sanders, Joe. "Vigorous, Messy, Untidy—And Compulsively Readable." *Fantasy Review* 76 (February, 1985): 17-18.

56. *Saturday Review* 10 (November, 1984): 85.

57. Schachtsiek-Freitag, Norbert. "Horror and Fantasy: Stephen Kings und Peter Straubs *Der Talisman.*" *Frankfurter Rundschau* [West Germany] 12 August 1986. German-language review.

58. Schulte, Jean. "Two Grim Reapers Predictably Macabre in Modern Dark Ages." *Columbus Dispatch* [OH] 4 November 1984. As microfiche: *NewsBank*: Literature 11 (December 1984): Fiche 58, A12.

59. Schweitzer, Darrell, ed. *Discovering Stephen King.* Mercer Island, WA: Starmont House, STARMONT STUDIES IN LITERARY CRITICISM #8, 1985, 219 pp., $17.95, hardcover. ISSN 0737-1306. ISBN 0-93-261-07-0. Issued simultaneously in paperback, $9.95, ISBN 0930261-06-2.

60. ———. "Epic Fantasy in Modern Dress." *Philadelphia Inquirer* 11 November 1984. As microfiche: *NewsBank*: Literature 11 (December 1984): Fiche 58, A13.

61. *Science Fiction Review* 14 (February, 1985): 41.

62. Shapiro, Anna. *New York Times Book Review* 89 (November 4, 1984): 24. Excerpted in: *Contemporary Literary Criticism*, Volume 37. Edited by Daniel G. Marowski. Detroit: Gale Research Co., 1986, hardcover. 205-206.

63. Sherman, David. "Nightmare Library." *Fangoria* no. 44 (1985): 39-40.

64. Shestak, George. "King/Straub Tale Overloads to a Point of Numbness." *Omaha World-Herald* 4 November 1984. As microfiche: *NewsBank*: Literature 11 (December, 1984): Fiche 58, A11.

65. Skow, John. *Time* 124 (November 5, 1984): 88.

66. Slay, Jack, Jr. "'The Road Laid Its Mark on You': Jack's Metamorphosis in *The Talisman* (or, Beyond Boy-Wonderdom)." *Castle Rock: The Stephen King Newsletter* 4:7 (July 1988): 1, 4-5.

67. Small, Michael. "Peter Straub & Stephen King Team Up for Fear." *People Weekly* (January 28, 1985): 50-52.

68. Smithers, Susan L. *School Library Journal* 31 (January 1985): 92.

69. Somerville, Richard. "Huck Meets Hobbit." *Des Moines Register* [IA] 4 November 1984. As microfiche: *NewsBank*: Literature 11

(December 1984): Fiche 58, A7.

70. Spignesi, Stephen J. "The Talisman." *The Shape Under the Sheet: The Complete Stephen King Encyclopedia.* Ann Arbor, MI: Popular Culture, Ink., May 1991, hardcover, p. 304-317.

71. Steinberg, Sylvia. "PW Forecasts: Fiction." *Publishers Weekly* 226 (September 7, 1984): 73. "This collaborative work by the two best-selling authors and close friends surpasses the expectations created by their separate past works.... Seamlessly written, *The Talisman* is a grand novel...."

72. Straub, Peter. "Straub Talks About *Talisman.*" *Castle Rock: The Stephen King Newsletter* 1:7 (July 1985): 1, 3.

73. Stuewe, Paul. 50 (December 24, 1984): 37.

74. Terrell, Carroll F. *Stephen King: Man and Artist.* Orono ME: Northern Lights Publications, 1990, hardcover. 219-238.

75. Toepfer, Susan. "'*The Talisman*': A Classic." *Daily News* [NY] 14 October 1984. As microfiche: *NewsBank*: Literature 11 (November, 1984): Fiche 46, A6-A7.

76. Tucker, Ken. "Boo! Ha-Ha, You Sap!" *The Village Voice* 29:43 (October 23, 1984): 53. Excerpted in: *Contemporary Literary Criticism*, Volume 37. Edited by Daniel G. Marowski. Detroit: Gale Research Co., 1986, hardcover, p. 205.

77. Turner, Billy. "King-Straub Combo Pleases, But Fails to Horrify." *Clarion-Ledger* [Jackson, MS] 21 October 1984. As microfiche: *NewsBank*: Literature 11 (November 1984): Fiche 46, A4.

78. Underwood, Tim, and Chuck Miller, eds. *Kingdom of Fear: The World of Stephen King.* Columbia, PA: Underwood-Miller, April 1986, trade paperback.

79. *USA Today* 3 (October 19, 1984): 3D.

80. *Village Voices Literary Supplement* (May 1993): 25+.

81. Wallace, Gail Smith. "Happy Halloween Horrors to You!" *News and Observer* [Raleigh, NC] 28 October 1984. As microfiche: *NewsBank*: Literature 11 (November 1984): Fiche 46, A8-A9.

82. *West Coast Review of Books* 11 (January 1985): 33.

83. Winter, Douglas E. Stephen King: *The Art of Darkness.* New York: New American Library, November 1984, 252 pp., $14.95, hardcover. ISBN 0-453-00476-8.

*WILD ANIMALS: THREE NOVELS—JULIA, IF YOU COULD SEE ME NOW,
UNDER VENUS.* New York: G. P. Putnam's Sons, October 1984.

A13.

Wild Animals:
Three Novels

Julia
If You COuld See Me Now

Under Venus
(1984)

A13. *WILD ANIMALS: THREE NOVELS—JULIA, IF YOU COULD SEE ME NOW, UNDER VENUS*. New York: G. P. Putnam's Sons, October 1984, 591 pp., $18.95, hardcover; single print-run of about 20,000 copies. ISBN 0-399-13013-6. Omnibus fiction collection, including *Julia, If You Could See Me Now,* and *Under Venus.*

b. *Under Venus.* New York: Berkeley, February 1985, 289 pp., $3.95, paperback reprint. ISBN 0-425-07033-6.

c. *Under Venus*: as *Bajo Venus* ['Under Venus']. Esplugas de Llobregat (Barcelona, Spain): Plaza & Janés Editores, September 1985, 288 pp., $12.95, paper. Spanish translation by Rosa S. Naviera. ISBN 84-01-32172-7.

d. *Under Venus* as: *Bajo Venus* ['Under Venus']. Esplugas de Llobregat (Barcelona, Spain): Plaza & Janés Editores, October 1986, 288 pp., 934 pta, trade paperback. Spanish translation by Rosa S. de Naviera. ISBN 84-01-32172-7.

e. *Under Venus*: as *Das Geheimnisvolle Mädchen* ['The Secretive Girl']. München, Germany: Wilhelm Heyne Verlag, HEYNE ALLGEMEINE REIHE (01) #09877, 1986, 348 pp., DM 12,90,

> paperback. German translation by Joachim Korber. ISBN 3-453-09967-2. Also published as: as *Das Geheimnisvolle Mädchen*. München, Germany: Wilhelm Heyne Verlag, 348 pp., DM 7,90, mass-market paperback. German translation by Joachim Korber. ISBN 3-453-02392-7..
>
> f. *Under Venus*: as *Bajo Venus* ['Under Venus']. 2nd edition. Esplugas de Llobregat (Barcelona, Spain): Plaza & Janés Editores, June 1991, 288 pp., 728 pta, paperback. Spanish translation by Rosa S. de Naviera. ISBN 84-01-49421-4.
>
> g. *Under Venus*: as *In Het Teken Van Venus*. Utrecht, Netherlands: Luitingh-Sijthoff, 288 pp., trade paperback. Dutch translation by Margot Bakker. ISBN 90-245-1736-2.
>
> h. *Wild Animals*. New York: Quality Paperback Book Club, Putnam, October 1985, 591 pp., [no price given], trade paperback reprint. Book Club Edition. No ISBN listed.

CONTENTS: "Introduction" [pp. 7-12]; *Julia* [pp. 15-177]; *If You Could See Me Now* [pp. 181-388]; *Under Venus* [pp. 391-591]

COMMENTS: *Under Venus* was written in 1973-74 but not published until its inclusion in *Wild Animals*.

SELECTED ARTICLES AND REVIEWS:
1. *Booklist* Vol. 80 (August 1984): 1601.
2. *Kirkus Reviews* Vol. 52 (1 August 1984): 710.
3. Eidus, Janice. *New York Times Book Review* Vol. 90 (24 March 1985): 15.
4. Johnson, Eric W. *Library Journal* Vol. 109 (1 October 1984): 1864.
5. Sanders, Joe. "Is the Child Father to the Man?" *Fantasy Review* Vol. 8, no. 2, Issue 76 (February 1985): 26. "Even though I can recommend only *Julia* as a wholly successful novel, I was impressed by Straub's writing skill and his determination to explore the soul's most desperately guarded secrets."
6. Steinberg, Sylvia. "PW Forecasts: Fiction." *Publishers Weekly* Vol. 226 (10 August 1984): 72-73.
7. *Village Voice* Vol. 29 (23 October 1984): 53.
8. *Village Voices Literary Supplement* (May 1993): 25+.
9. Winter, Douglas E. "A Sorcerer's Apprentice." *Washington Post Book World* Vol. 14, no. 42 (14 October 1984): 1-2. "*Wild Animals* is not only splendid entertainment, but also a worthy case history in the making of a modern writer" (2).

BLUE ROSE. San Francisco CA, Columbia PA: Underwood-Miller,
September 1985.

A14.

Blue Rose (1985)

A14. *BLUE ROSE*. San Francisco CA, Columbia PA: Underwood-Miller, September 1985, 92 pp., $35.00, limited slipcased edition, 600 copies [perhaps 350 actually printed]. Jacket design by Ned Dameron. ISBN 0-88733-005-3. Novella. [See also B5]

  b. In: *Cutting Edge.* Edited by Dennis Etchison. Garden City NY: Doubleday & Company, October 1986, 290 pp., $16.95, hardcover. 1-51. ISBN 0-385-234530-9.

  c. In: *Cutting Edge.* Edited by Dennis Etchison. London: Macdonald & Co., 1986, 290 pp., £11.95, hardcover. ISBN 0-356-15154-9.

  d. As: *Blaue Rose* ['Blue Rose']. Bellheim, Germany: Edition Phantasia, 1986. 102 pp., 78,00 DM, hardcover; limited edition of 250 copies. First German Edition. Illustrated by Uwe Mayer. German translation by Joachim Körber. ISBN 3-924959-03-X.

  e. In: *Cutting Edge.* Edited by Dennis Etchison. London: Futura, 1987, 290 pp., £2.95, paperback. ISBN 0-7088-3608-9.

  f. In: *Houses without Doors* London: Grafton, 1990. [A16].

  g. Rpt. in: *Superhorror: Vier ungekurzte Romane* ['Superhorror: Four Unabridged Novels']. München, Germany: Wilhelm Heyne Verlag, 1990, 778 pp., dm 10,00. Paperback. ISBN 3-453-04241-7.

  h. In: *Foundations of Fear.* Edited by David G. Hartwell. New York: Tor, September 1992, 660 pp., $27.50, hardcover. 163-196. Short fiction by Straub, H. P. Lovecraft, Clive Barker, Daphne Du Maurier, Robert A. Heinlein, Richard Matheson, and others. ISBN 0-312-85074-3.

  i. In: *Shadows of Fear: Foundations of Fear, Volume I..* Edited by David G. Hartwell. New York: Tor, June 1994, 468 pp., $4.99, paperback reprint. 335-400. ISBN 0-812-51896-9.

  j. As: *Blue Rose.* New York: Penguin, August 1995, 87 pp., $.95, trade paperback; published as one of sixty short-story paperbacks to celebrate Penguin's sixtieth anniversary ("Penguin 60); cover art by Charles Burchfield. ISBN 0-14-600107-9.

SELECTED ARTICLES AND REVIEWS:

1. Morrison, Michael A. "Hypnosis Made Easy." *Fantasy Review* Vol. 9, #90 (April 1986): 28-29. "*Blue Rose* is a horrifying guided tour of the mind of a sadistic child .... *Blue Rose* exhibits all the hallmarks of Straub's novels—carefully wrought prose, vividly drawn characters and subtle psychological insights. But this novella lacks the novels' complexity; lean, cold, and sharp as a scalpel, it has a power and precision that reminds me of Graham Green's (very different) portrayal of evil in *Brighton Rock*"

PETER
STRAUB
BLUE ROSE

p e n g u i n   6 0 s

Blue Rose. New York: Penguin, August 1995.

Koko. New York: E. P. Dutton, October 1988.

A15.
Koko (1988)

A15. *KOKO.* New York: E. P. Dutton, October 1988, xi+562 pp., $19.95, hardcover, 40,000 copies. ISBN 0-525-24660-6. Novel.

b. London: Viking (UK), October 1988, 562 pp., £12.95, hardcover. First British Edition. ISBN 0-670-80131-3.

c. New York: Quality Paperback Book Club, January 1989, $9.95, 562 pp., trade paperback. No ISBN listed.

d. London: Penguin Overseas, May 1989, 625 pp., £3.99, paperback reprint. Not available in Britain. ISBN 0-14-007187-3.

e. New York: Signet, June 1989, [not for sale], 595 pp. paperback. Distributed at the ABA only. ISBN 0-451-16208-0.

f. London: Penguin, June 1989, 635 pp., £3.99, paperback. ISBN 0-14-007187-3.

g. New York: Signet/NAL-Dutton, October/November 1989, 595 pp., $5.95, trade paperback. ISBN 0-451-16214-5.

h. As: *Koko*. Barcelona, Spain: Ediciones B, S.A., ÉXITO INTERNACIONAL #24, October 1989, 616 pp., 2233 pta, hardcover. Spanish translation by Hernan Sabate. ISBN 84-406-0988-4.

i. As: *Koko*. München, Germany: Wilhelm Heyne Verlag, 1989, 559 pp., DM 24,80. German translation by Uta McKechneay. ISBN 3-453-00373-X.

j. As: *Koko*. Utrecht, Netherlands: Uitgeverij Luitingh, 1989, 527 pp., paperback. Dutch translation by Margot Bakker. ISBN 90-245-1634-X.

k. As: *Koko*. Paris, France: Éditions Robert Laffont, BEST SELLERS, January 1990, 549 pp., 125.00FF/19.06 Euro, hardcover. French translation by Bernard Feny. Illustrated by Bob wood. ISBN 2-221-05725-2.

l. As: *Koko*. Stockholm, Norstedt, 1990, 560 pp., 240 SEK (Swedish Kronor), hardback. Swedish translation by Staffan Andrae. ISBN 9118922724.

m. As: *Koko* (Blue Rose I). Paris, France: Presses Pocket,

TERREUR # 9047, March 1991, 608 pp., 41.00ff/6.25 Euro, paperback. French translation by Bernard Feny. Illustrated by Kéna. ISBN 2-266-03884-2. Reissued: 1994.

n. As: *Koko.* Milano, Italy: Sperling & Kupfer, PANDORA BESTSELLER, 1991, 568 pp., L 28.900 [$], hardcover. Italian translation by Sofia Mohamed. ISBN 88-7824-594-1.

o. As: *Koko.* Barcelona, Spain: Ediciones B, S.A., VIB #3/1, March 1992, 832 pp., 1140 pta, paperback. Spanish translation by Hernan Sabaté Vargas. ISBN 84-406-2722-X.

p. As: *Koko.* Stockholm, MånPocket, 1992, 560 pp., 59:50 SEK (Swedish Kronor), paperback. Swedish translation by Staffan Andrae. ISBN 9176426947.

q. As: *Koko.* __, Spain: RBA Coleccionables, S.A., GRANDES ÉXITOS #81, November 1994, 592 pp., 966 pta. Spanish translation by Hernán Sabaté. ISBN 84-473-0629-1.

r. As: *Koko.* __, Finland: Book Studio Oy, 1994. Finnish translation by Annika Eräpuroa.

s. New York: Signet, July 1995, $6.99, paperback reissue. ISBN 0-451-16214-5.

t. As: *Koko.* Milano, Italy: Sperling & Kupfer, May 1996, 570 pp., L. 15.000 [#7.26], paperback. Italian translation.

u. Praha-Plzen, Czech Republic: Beta/Dobrovsky & Sevcik, 1998, 527 pp., 285 CZK. Czech translation by Ivo Reitmayer; cover art by Michal Houba. ISBN 80-86029-49-2.

v. As: *Koko.* Paris: Éditions Robert Laffont608 pp., paperback. French translation by Bernard Feny. ISBN 2-266-03884-2.

w. As: *Koko.* Japan: Kadokawa, 467 pp., 1000 Y, paperback. ISBN 4-04-265802-4.

x. As audiotape: Simon & Schuster Audio, November 1988, $14.95, 2 cassettes. Read by James Woods. ISBN 0671652397.

y. As calendar: *Koko.* New York: Dutton, 19__. ISBN 1-111-20274-5. [Reported in an Internet reference, but not verified]

COMMENTS: Received Best Novel, World Fantasy Awards, 1989.

SELECTED ARTICLES AND REVIEWS:
1. *Booklist* Vol. 84 (July 1988): 1756.
2. *Books* November 1988: 21. [Formerly *Books & Bookmen*]
3. Campbell, Don G. "Storytellers: New in October." *Los Angeles Times Book Review* 18 September 1988: 10.
4. Chow, Dan. "*Koko,* Peter Straub." *Locus* Vol. 21, No. 12, Issue 335

(December 1988). Review.

5. De Lint, Charles. "Straub's Vietnam Thriller Lacks His Usual Literary Strength." *The Ottawa Citizen* 2 October 1988. Review.

6. Dziemianowicz, Stephen (with Michael Morrison). "The Year in Horror. 1988—Horror with a Human Face: Harris and Straub." *Science Fiction & Fantasy Book Review Annual, 1989*. Edited by Robert A. Collins and Robert Latham. Westport CT: Meckler, 1990, hardcover. 73-75. ISBN 0-88736-369-5. "Amazingly, Straub infuses new life into a theme that would seem done to death: the psychotic Vietnam vet. His success flows from the novel's powerful philosophical subtext: the quest for values by one who has seen moral absolutes swept away" (74). Essay

7. *Emergency Librarian* Vol. 19 (September 1991): 59.

8. Fuller, Richard. *New York Times Book Review* Vol. 93 (9 October 1988): 34.

9. *Inside Books* May 1989: 79. Review of audio version.

10. Johnson, George. "New & Noteworthy." *New York Times Book Review* Vol. 94 (17 December 1989): 32.

11. *Kirkus Reviews* Vol. 56 (1 July 1988): 929.

12. *Kliatt Young Adult Paperback Book Guide* Vol. 24 9April 1990): 20.

13. *Magazine of Fantasy and Science Fiction* Vol. 75 (December 1988): 18.

14. *New Statesman & Society* Vol. 3 (7 December 1990): 34.

15. Norton, Nik. *Vector* #147 (December 1988). Review [British].

16. Steinberg, Sylvia. "PW Forecasts: Fiction." *Publishers Weekly* Vol. 234 (12 August 1988): 438. "...[H]is most gripping, most hallucinogenic thriller to date....The characters are realistic and complex, and the story continues to resonate in the mind long after the final page is turned."

17. *Publishers Weekly* Vol. 236 (13 October 1989): 50.

18. *Quill & Quire* [Canada] Vol. 55 (April 1989): 24. Review of audio version.

19. Ridge, Putney Tyson, Ph.D. (pseudonym for Straub). "*Koko*." Online: http://net-site.com/straub/pt_koko.htm.

20. Schuyler, William W., Jr. Review. *Science Fiction & Fantasy Book Review Annual, 1989*. Edited by Robert A. Collins and Robert Latham. Westport CT: Meckler, 1990. 415. 0-88736-369-5.

21. Shepard, Lucius. "Stalking the Nightmare." *Washington Post Book World* Vol. 18 (21 August 1988): 3.

22. *Tribune Books* [Chicago IL] 2 October 1988: 6.

23. *Village Voices Literary* Supplement (May 1993): 25+.

24. *Voice of Youth Advocates* Vol. 13 (June 1990): 138.

Houses without Doors. London: Grafton, October 1990.

A16.

Houses Without Doors (1990)

A16. *HOUSES WITHOUT DOORS.* London: Grafton, October 1990, 303 pp., £13.99, hardcover. Cover art by Peter Goodfellow. Simultaneous with the American Dutton edition [L. W. Curry places this edition one month earlier than the Dutton]. ISBN 0-246-13759-2. Short-fiction and novella collection.

b. New York: E. P. Dutton [NAL], October/November 1990, vii+358 pp., $19.95, hardcover, 15,000 copies. Cover art by Rob Wood. ISBN 0-525-24924-9.

c. New York: Book-of-the-Month Club, November 1990, 356 pp., $17.95, hardcover. Cover art by Rob Wood. No ISBN listed.

d. New York: Book-of-the-Month Club/Quality Paperback Book Club, July 1991, 356 pp., $9.95, trade paperback. Book Club Edition.. No ISBN listed.

e. London: Grafton Overseas, September 1991, 448 pp., £4.50, paperback. Cover art by Stuart Bodek. Distributed only in non-English-speaking countries. ISBN 0-586-21202-7.

f. As: *Duistere Visioenen* ['Dark Visions']. Utrecht, Netherlands: Uitgeverij Luitingh, 1991, 343 pp., paperback. Dutch translation by Frank Visser. ISBN 90-245-1969-1.

g. New York: Signet/NAL-Dutton, November 1991, 454 pp., $5.99, mass-market paperback. ISBN 0-451-17082-2.

h. London: Grafton, April 1992, 448 pp., £4.99, paperback. Cover art by Stuart Bodek. ISBN 0-586-21202-7.

i. As: *Casa sin puertas* ['House without Doors']. Barcelona, Spain: Ediciones B, S.A., April 1992, 384 pp., 2330 pta, paperback. Spanish translation by M. Magdalena Ferrer. ISBN 84-406-2541-3.

j. As: *Sans portes ni fenêtres* ['Neither Doors Nor Windows']. Paris, France: Olivier Orban, October 1992, 382 pp., 135.00 FF, hardcover. French translation by Gérard Coisne. Illustrated by Rob Wood. ISBN 2-855645-708-3.

Contents: "Blue Rose"; "Le Genévrier" ("The Juniper Tree"); "Petit guide à l'usage des touristes" ("A Short Guide to the City"); "Le Chasseur de bisons" ("The Buffalo Hunter"); "Où l'on voit la mort et aussi des flammes" ("Something About a Death, Something About a Fire"); "Mme Dieu" ("Mrs. God")

k. As: *Casa sin puertas* ['House without Doors']. Barcelona, Spain: Círculo de Lectores, S.A., February 1993, 368 pp., 1553 pta, hardcover. Spanish translation by M. Magdalena Ferrer. ISBN 84-226-4386-3.

l. As: *Casa sin puertas* ['House without Doors']. Barcelona, Spain: Ediciones B, S.A., April 1993, 528 pp., 895 pta, paperback. Spanish translation by Peralta Ferrer and Magdalena Ferrer. ISBN 84-406-3687-3.

m. London: Grafton, June 1993, 448 pp., £4.99, paperback. Cover art by Melvyn Grant. ISBN 0-586-21202-7.

n. As: *Haus ohne Türen* ['House without Doors']. München, Germany: Wilhelm Heyne Verlag, HEYNE JUMBO BÄNDE #41, 00045; 1993, dm 26,80; hardcover. German translation. ISBN 3-453-06247-7.

o. As: *Sans portes, ni fenêtres* ['Neither Doors Nor Windows']. Paris, France: Pocket, TERREUR #9106, January 1994, 382 pp., 35.00 FF/5.34 Euro, paperback. 6 nouvelles. French translation by Gérard Coisne. Illustrated by Pierre-Olivier Templier. ISBN 2-266-05737-5.

Contents: "Blue Rose"; "Le Genévrier" ("The Juniper Tree"); "Petit guide à l'usage des touristes" ("A Short Guide to the City"); "Le Chasseur de bisons" ("The Buffalo Hunter"); "Où l'on voit la mort et aussi des flammes" ("Something About a Death, Something About a Fire"); "Mme Dieu" ("Mrs. God").

p. As: *Haus Ohne Türen* ['House without Doors']. München, Germany: Wilhelm Heyne Verlag, 1994, 446 pp., dm 12,90; paperback. German translation by Andreas Brandhorst. ISBN 3-453-07551-X.

q. As: *Houses Without Doors*. Japan: Fusosha, 1995, 613 pp., 1900 Y, hardcover. ISBN. 4-594-01653-7.

r. As: *Haus Ohne Türen* ['House without Doors']. Augsburg, Germany: Bechtermunz Verlag. 1996, 446 pp., hardcover. German translation by Andreas Brandhorst. ISBN 3-86047-522-3.

s. As audiotape: *Houses Without Doors,* Simon & Schuster, August 1990. 2 cassettes. Read by Will Patton. Includes "Blue Rose" and "A Short Guide to the City," unabridged.

t. As calendar: *Houses Without Doors.* New York: Dutton, 19__. ISBN 1-299-81917-6. [Reported on the Internet, but not verified.]

CONTENTS: "She Saw a Young Man" [See B13]; "Blue Rose" [See A14, B5]; "Interlude: In the Realm of Dreams" [See B9]; "The Juniper Tree" [See B3]; "Interlude: Going Home" [See B8]; "A Short Guide to the City" [See B14]; "Interlude: The Poetry Reading" [See B10]; "The Buffalo Hunter" [See B6]; "Interlude: Bar Talk" [See B7]; "Something about Death, Something about a Fire" [See B15]; "Interlude: The Veteran" [See B11]; "Mrs. God" [See A17, B4, B12]; "Then One Day She Saw Him Again" [See B16]; "Author's Note" [See C6]

COMMENTS: "The Juniper Tree" first appeared in *Prime Evil,* edited by Douglas E. Winter [see B3]; all other stories are original to this volume.

SELECTED ARTICLES AND REVIEWS:
1. *Bloomsbury Review* Vol. 11 (December 1991): 27.
2. *Booklist* Vol. 87 (15 January 1991): 1008.
3. *Book Watch* Vol. 12 (March 1991): 4.
4. *Book Watch* Vol. 13 (May 1992): 9. Review of audio version.
5. Campbell, Dan G. *Los Angeles Times Book Review* (18 November 1990): 6.
6. Chow, Dan. "*Houses without Doors,* Peter Straub." *Locus,* 25:6, no 359 (December 1990): 21. Review.
7. Collings, Michael R. *Mystery Scene* No. 28 (January 1991): 90. "Cerebral, abstracted, often symbolic and difficult, just as often highly literary and frustratingly allusive, the novellas that comprise *Houses Without Doors* nevertheless testify to Straub's mastery of substance and style. Never easy, rarely straightforward, the stories impel the reader into worlds of distorted vision and imagination and violence and death."
8. —. *SFRA Newsletter* [Science Fiction Research Association], No. 193 (December 1991): 64-65.
9. —. *Science Fiction & Fantasy Book Review Annual 1991,* Edited by Robert A. Collins and Robert Latham. Westport CT: Greenwood Press, 1993, 532.

10. Graeber, Laurel. "New & Noteworthy." *New York Times Book Review* Vol. 96 (17 November 1991): 34.
11. Kendrick, Walter. "Guts and Brains." *The New York Times Book Review.* 30 December, 1990: VIII, 6.
12. *Kirkus Reviews* Vol. 58 (15 August 1990): 1126.
13. Lehmann-Haupt, Christopher. *The New York Times* 24 December 1990: I, 19.
14. *Locus* Vol. 25 (December 1990): 55.
15. *Locus* Vol. 26 (January 1991): 59.
16. *Locus* Vol. 26 (February 1991): 35.
17. *Locus* Vol. 27 (August 1991): 52.
18. *Locus* Vol. 27 (December 1991): 56.
19. Miller, Faren. "*Houses without Doors*, Peter Straub." *Locus,* 25:2, no. 355 (August 1990): 15. Review.
20. *New Statesman & Society* Vol. 3 (7 December 1990): 34.
21. Ridge, Putney Tyson, Ph.D. (pseudonym for Straub). "*Houses Without Doors.*" Online: http://net-site.com/straub/pt_hous. htm.
22. *Science Fiction Chronicle* Vol. 12 (October 1990): 34.
23. Steinberg, Sybil. "PW Forecasts: Fiction." *Publishers Weekly* Vol. 237 (5 October 1990): 88. "This collection...reveals Straub at his spellbinding best....Straub's fictions are playfully postmodern, resonating with insights on genre, craft and process."
24. *Village Voice Literary Supplement* (May 1993): 25+.
25. *Voice of Youth Advocates* Vol. 15 (June 1992): 144.
26. *Washington Post Book World* Vol. 20 (28 October 1990): 1.
27. *World & I* (Washington DC)Vol. 6 (August 1991): 472.
28. *New York Times Late Edition* 24 December 1990: 19.

MRS. GOD. Hampton Falls NH: Donald M. Grant, December
1990/January 1991

A17.

Mrs. God (1990)

A17. *MRS. GOD.* Hampton Falls NH: Donald M. Grant, December 1990/January 1991, 206 pp., $30.00, hardcover, slipcased trade edition of 600 copies. Afterword by Straub; illustrations by Rick Berry. ISBN 0-937986-97-6. Novella [See also A16, B4, B12]

    b. Hampton Falls NH: Donald M. Grant, 1990, 195 pp., $65.00, signed deluxe edition, [announced]. ISBN 0-937986-96-8.

    c. As audiotape: *Mrs. God,* Simon & Schuster Audio, November 1991, $16.00, unabridged. 2 cassettes. Read by Kevin Spacey. ISBN 0671748793.

SELECTED ARTICLES AND REVIEWS:

1. *Book Watch* Vol. 12 (May 1991): 3.
2. Chow, Dan. "*Mrs. God*, Peter Straub." *Locus* Vol. 27, No. 3, Issue 368 (September 1991). Review.
3. *Kliatt Young Adult Paperback Book Guide* Vol. 26 (September 1992): 59. Review of audio version.
4. *Locus* Vol. 26 (April 1991): 44.
5. *Necrofile: The Review of Horror Fiction* (Summer 1991): 23.
6. Ridge, Putney Tyson, Ph.D. (pseudonym for Straub). "*Mrs. God.*" Online: http://net-site.com/straub/pt_god.htm.
7. *Science Fiction Chronicle* Vol. 12 (May 1991): 33.
8. *Washington Post Book World* Vol. 21 (28 April 1991): 8.

PETER STRAUB

I KNOW WHAT YOU ARE

MYSTERY

A novel by the author of Ghost Story and Koko

MYSTERY. New York: E. P. Dutton, November 1990.

A18.

Mystery *(1990)*

A18. *MYSTERY.* New York: E. P. Dutton, November 1990, 548 pp., $19.95, hardcover, 40,000 copies. Cover art by Paul Bacon. ISBN 0-525-24818-8. Novel.

   b. London: Grafton Overseas, December 1990, 548 pp., £4.50, paperback. Cover art by Alun Hood. Not distributed in Britain. ISBN 0-586-20958-1.

   c. London: Grafton, February 1990, 548 pp., £13.95, hardcover. Cover art by Alun Hood. ISBN 0-246-13655-3.

   d. London: Grafton Overseas, June 1990, 548 pp., £4.50, paperback. Cover art by Alun Hood. Not generally distributed in Britain. ISBN 0-586-20958-1.

   e. As: *Misterio.* Barcelona, Spain, Ediciones B, S.A., ÉXITOS INTERNACIONAL #40, November 1990, 580 pages, 2427 pta, hardcover. Spanish translation by Antoni Puigrós Jaume. ISBN 84-406-1784-4.

   f. As: *Mystery.* München, Germany: Wilhelm Heyne Verlag, 1990, 525 pp., DM 26,80, paperback. German translation by Joachim Korber. ISBN 3-453-04675-7.

   g. As: *Komplot* ['Plot']. Utrecht, Netherlands: Uitgeverij Luitingh-Sijthoff, 1990, 479 pp., trade paperback. Dutch translation by Elly Schurisk-Vooren. ISBN 90-245-1730-3.

   h. New York: Penguin/Signet, January 1991, 545 pp., $5.95, paperback. ISBN 0-451-16869-0. 7th printing by 1999.

   i. As: *Mystery.* Paris, France: Editions Olivier Orban, February 1991, 511 pp., 149.00 FF, hardcover. French translation by Gérard Coisne. Illustrated by Rob Wood. Graphics by Jérôme Lo Monaco. ISBN 2-85565-632-X.

   j. London: Grafton, April 1991, 548 pp., £4.99, paperback. Cover art by Alun Hood. . ISBN 0-586-20958-1.

   k. As: *Misterio.* Barcelona, Spain: Círculo de Lectores, S. A., July 1991, 592 pp., 1533 pta, hardcover. Spanish translation by Antoni Puigrós. ISBN 84-226-3667-0.

l. As: *Mistery.* Milano, Italy: Sperling & Kupfer, NARRATIVA, 1991, 544 pp., L28.900 [$13.99]. Italian translation.

m. As: *Myethpio.* Athens: Bell, 1991, 571 pp., 850Apx., paperback. Greek translation by Llayvqu Iouvqidov.

n. As: *Tudom Ki Vagy.* Budapest, Hungary: Maecenas International, 1991, 418 pp., 189Ft, paperback. Hungarian translation by Odze Gyorgy. ISBN 963-782-713-7.

o. As: *Misterio.* Barcelona, Spain: Ediciones B, S.A., VIB 3/2, October 1992, 719 pp., 966 pta, paperback. Spanish translation by Antoni Puigrós. ISBN 84-406-3418.8.

p. As: *Mystery.* Paris, France: Pocket, TERREUR #9088, October 1992, 511 pp., 48.00FF/7.32 Euro, paperback. French translation by Gérard Coisne. Illustrated by Pierre-Olivier Templier. ISBN 2-266-05275-6. Reissued, 1996.

q. As: *Misterio os Crimes da Rosa Azul* ['Mystery, the Crimes of the Blue Rose']. Rio de Janeiro, Brazil: Francisco Alves, 1992, 422 pp., paperback. Portuguese translation by Luisa Ibanez and Sylvio Goncalves. ISBN 85-265-0284-0.

r. As: *Mysterier.* Copenhagen, Denmark: Artia, 1992, 522 pp., hardcover. Danish translation by Modens Wenzel Anderason. ISBN 87-89294-66-1.

s. London: Grafton, June 1993, 548 pp., £5.99, paperback. Cover art by Melvyn Grant. ISBN 0-586-20958-1.

t. As: *Mystery.* Japan: Fusosha, 1994, 509 pp., 1800 Y, hardcover. ISBN 4-594-01418-6.

u. As: *Mistery.* Milano, Italy: Sperling, May 1995, 536 pp., L 15.00 [$7.26], paperback. Italian translation.

v. As: *Mystery.* Japan: Fusosha, 1995, 503 pp., 680 Y, paperback. ISBN 4-594-02686-3.

w. New York: Signet, January 1997, $7.99, mass-market paperback reissue. ISBN 0451168690.

x. As: *Mystery* (Blue Rose-2). Paris, France: Pocket, #9088, 1992, paperback. French translation.

y. As audiotape: Simon & Schuster Audioworks, February 1990, $14.95, abridged, 2 cassettes, 180 minutes. Read by James Woods. ISBN 0-671-69268-2.

SELECTED ARTICLES AND REVIEWS:
1. AB Bookman's Weekly Vol. 85 (23 April 1990): 1735.
2. Booklist Vol. 86 (1 November 1989): 499.
3. Booklist Vol. 86 (15 May 1990): 1826. Review of audio version.

4. Kaganoff, P. "Forecasts: Paperback." *Publishers Weekly* Vol. 237 (7 December 1990): 80. "Reprint Fiction" note.
5. Key, Samuel M. Review. *Science Fiction & Fantasy Book Review Annual, 1990.* Edited by Robert A. Collins and Robert Latham. New York: Greenwood Press, 1991. 461. 0-313-28150-5
6. *Kirkus Reviews* Vol. 57 (1 November 1989): 1559.
7. *Kliatt Young Adult Paperback Book Guide* Vol. 25 (April 1991): 15.
8. *Los Angeles Times Book Review* 9 December 1990: 14.
9. *Locus* Vol. 24 (January 1990): 15.
10. *Locus* Vol. 24 (January 1990): 53.
11. *Locus* Vol. 26 (February 1991): 60.\
12. Miller, Faren. "*Mystery,* Peter Straub." *Locus* 24:1, no. 348 (January 1990). Review.
13. Nathan, Paul. "Fresh Start." *Publishers Weekly* Vol. 243, No. 37 (9 September 1996): 32. Discussion of acquisition of television rights to *Mystery* by New Amsterdam Entertainment.
14. *Publishers Weekly* Vol. 237 (2 March 1990): 60. Review of audio version.
15. Ridge, Putney Tyson, Ph.D. (pseudonym for Straub). "*Mystery.*" Online: http://net-site.com/straub/pt_myst.htm.
16. Steinberg, Sylvia. "PW Forecasts: Fiction." *Publishers Weekly* Vol. 236 (10 November 1989): 51.
17. *Tribune Books* [Chicago IL] 20 January 1991): 12.
18. *Village Voices Literary* Supplement (May 1993): 25+.
19. *Washington Post Book World* Vol. 20 (11 February 1990): 1.
20. *West Coast Review of Books* Vol. 15, #3 (1990): 32.

THE THROAT. New York: E. P. Dutton [NAL], April 1993.

A19.

The Throat (1993)

A19. *THE THROAT.* New York: E. P. Dutton [NAL], April 1993, 689 pp., $24.00, hardcover, about 30,000 copies. Cover art by Rob Wood. ISBN 0-525-93503-7. Novel.

b. Grantham NH: Borderlands, March 1993, 689 pp., $100.00, signed, slipcased edition of 500 (600?) copies. Flap copy by Putney Tyson Ridge (pseudonym For Straub).

c. As: *La Garganta* ['The Throat']. Esplugas de Llobregat (Barcelona, Spain): Plaza & Janés, S.A., PLAZA Y JANÉS ÉXITOS, March 1993, 696 pp., 2767 pta, hardcover. Spanish translation by Ana María de la Fuente. ISBN 84-01-32503-X.

d. New York: Book-of-the-Month Club, April, 1993, 689 pp., $19.95, hardcover. Cover art by Rob Wood. No ISBN listed.

e. London: HarperCollins UK, June 1993, 689 pp., £15.99, hardcover. Cover art by Pam Ronsaville. First British Edition. ISBN 0-00-224178-1.

f. As: [*Der*] *Schlund* ['The Throat']. Wien [Vienna], Austria: Paul Zsolnay Verlag, October 1993, 587 pp., DM 46,00, hardcover. German translation by Edith Walter. ISBN 3-552-04527-8.

g. New York: Book-of-the-Month Club; Quality Paperback Book Club, December 1993, 689 pp., $12.95, trade paperback. Cover art by Rob Wood. Book Club Edition. . No ISBN listed.

h. As: *La Garganta* ['The Throat']. Barcelona, Spain: Círculo Lectores, S.A., December 1993, 696 pp., 2233 pta, hardcover. Spanish translation by Ana María de la Fuente. ISBN 84-226-4739-7.

i. As: *La garganta* ['The Throat']. Esplugas de Llobregat (Barcelona, Spain): Plaza & Janés, S.A., BIBLIOTECA DE PETER STRAUB #5, January 1994, 800 pp., 1165 pta, paperback. Spanish translation by Ana María de la Fuente. ISBN 84-01-49425-7.

j. As: *La garganta* ['The Throat']. Esplugas de Llobregat (Barcelona, Spain): Plaza & Janés, S.A., JET, January 1994,

800 pp., 1200 pta, paperback. Spanish translation by Ana María de la Fuente. ISBN 84-01-49160-6..

k. New York: Signet/NAL-Dutton March 1994, 697 pp., $6.99, mass-market paperback reprint edition. ISBN 0-451-17918-8.

l. London: HarperCollins UK, May 1994, 875 pp., £5.99, paperback. ISBN 0-586-21849-1.

m. As: *The Throat.* 2 vols. Russia, 1994, 431 pp. (Vol. 1), 447 pp., (vol. 2), paperback. ISBN 954-530-016-6 (vol.1), 954-530-016-7. (vol. 2).

n. As *La Gorge* ['The Throat']. Paris, France: Editions Plon, March 1995, 651 pp., 149.00 FF, hardcover. French translation by Jean Rosenthal. Illustrated by Rob Wood. Graphics by Pierre-Olivier Templier. ISBN 2-259-00-147-5.

o. As: *Der Schlund* ['The Throat']. München, Germany: Wilhelm Heyne Verlag, HEYNE ALLGEMEINE REIHE #09441, 1995, DM 14,90; paperback. German translation by Edith Walter. ISBN 3-453-08235-4.

p. As *La Gorge*['The Throat']. Paris, France: Editions Plon, 1995, 867 pp., mass-market paperback. French translation by Jean Rosenthal. ISBN 2-266-07220-X.

q. As: *La Gorge* (Blue Rose-3) ['The Throat']. Paris, France: Editions Pocket, TERREUR #9063, June 1996, 651 pp., 50.00 FF. French translation by Jean Rosenthal. Illustrated by Pierre-Olivier Templier. ISBN 2-266-07220-X.

r. As: *Suroto.* 2 vols. Japan: Fusosha, 1996, 462 pp. (vol. 1), 442 pp. (vol.2), 4000 Y, hardcover. ISBN 4-594-01940-4 (Vol. 1), 4-594-01941-2 (Vol. 2).

o. As: *Het kwaa* ['The Harm']. Amsterdam, Netherlands: Luitingh-Sijthoff, fl 15.00. Dutch translation. ISBN 9024524253.

p. As audiotape: Simon & Schuster Audio, April 1993, $25.00, abridged, 4 cassettes, 6 hours.. Read by William H. Macy. ISBN 0-671-72591-2.

COMMENTS: The novel, a sequel to *Koko* and *Mystery* in the 'Blue Rose' series, received the Bram Stoker Best Novel Award, Horror Writers of America, 1993. The hardcover edition was preceded by a pamphlet excerpt, with cover illustration, of 48 pages, distributed before publication to bookstores.

SELECTED ARTICLES AND REVIEWS:
1. *Book Watch* Vol. 14 (July 1993): 11.
2. *Book Watch* Vol. 15 (April 1994): 9. Review of audio version.
3. *Booklist* Vol. 89 (15 January 1993): 852.
4. *Books* Vol. 8 (May 1994): 15. [Formerly *Books & Bookmen*]
5. Graeber, Laurel. "New & Noteworthy." *New York Times Book Review* Vol. 99 (13 March 1994): 28.
6. *The Guardian Weekly* Vol. 148 (6 June 1993): 18.
7. *Kirkus Reviews* Vol. 61 (1 February 1993): 104. Online: Amazon.com At a Glance.
8. *Kliatt Young Adult Paperback Book Guide* Vol. 27 (July 1993): 48. Review of audio version.
9. *Locus* Vol. 32 (February 1994): 39+
10. *Locus* Vol. 32 (February 1994): 60.
11. *Locus* Vol. 32 (April 1994): 50.
12. Lyons, Gene. "Throttled." *Entertainment Weekly* No. 170 (14 May 1993): 50.
13. *Necrofile: The Review of Horror Fiction* (Summer 1993): 4+.
14. *Publishers Weekly* Vol. 241 (31 January 1994): 84. "Fiction Reprints" note.
15. Reagan, Reilly. "Audio Reviews." *Library Journal* Vol. 118 (15 April 1993): 149. Review of audio version.
16. Ridge, Putney Tyson, Ph.D. (pseudonym for Straub). *"The Throat:* A Friend's Observations." Online: http://net-site.com/straub/Put_Thr.htm.
17. Steinberg, Sybil. "PW Forecasts: Fiction." *Publishers Weekly* Vol. 240 (11 January 1993): 51. "Straub peaks with this visceral thriller.... Painted from a darkly colorful palette, Straub's characters inhabit a razor-edged world of unremitting suspense."
18. *Village Voices Literary Supplement* (May 1993): 25+.
19. Wallace, Jon. *Vector* (England) #174 (August 1993).
20. *Washington Post Book World* Vol. 23 (16 May 1993): 5+.
21. Wilson, Frank. *New York Times Book Review* Vol. 98 (27 June 1993): 24.

THE THROAT. Grantham NH: Borderlands, March 1993.

GHOSTS. NH: Borderlands Press, May 1995.

A20.

Peter Straub's

Ghosts

Horror Writers

of America Anthology

(1995)

A20. *PETER STRAUB'S GHOSTS*. Edited by Peter Straub. New York, London: Pocket Star Books [Pocket Books/Simon & Schuster], April 1995, 312 pp., $5.99, mass-market paperback. Cover art by Kirk Reinert. ISBN 0-671-88599-5. Horror Writers of America Anthology; original anthology of fifteen stories.

    b. As: *Ghosts*. Edited by Peter Straub. Grantham NH: Borderlands Press, May 1995, 302 pp., $65.00, slipcased, signed, and numbered edition of 350. Flap copy by Putney Tyson Ridge (pseudonym for Straub). Cover art by Rick Lieder. No ISBN listed.

CONTENTS: Peter Straub, "Hunger: An Introduction," pp. 1-41. [See B22]

    DARK: Norman Partridge, "Styx," pp. 45-58; Kathe Koja, "Jubilee," pp. 59-66; Tim Smith, "Not Far From Here," pp. 67-79;

    THE KIDS: Alan Rodgers, "Momma Ghost," pp. 83-106; Gordon R. Ross, "Daddy's Girl," pp. 107-118; Chet Williamson, "Coventry Carol," pp. 119-145;

    MOM AND DAD: David B. Silva, "And He Who Mourns," pp. 149-167; Clark Perry, "His Mother's Hands," pp. 168-185;

    COLD: Tyson Blue, "Bill Smith's Sleigh Ride (A Winter's Tale)," pp. 189-194; Lawrence Greenberg, "Sotto Voce," pp. 195-205; Brad Linaweaver, "A Real Babe," pp. 206-215;

OUR WORK: Thomas F. Monteleone, "Looking for Mr. Flip," pp. 219-253; Don D'Ammassa, "Present in Spirit," pp. 254-269; Paul M. Sammon, "The Wedding Party," pp. 270-307;
THE AUTHORS, pp. 309-312.

SELECTED ARTICLES AND REVIEWS:
1. Bryant, Edward. *"Peter Straub's Ghosts,* Peter Straub." *Locus* 34:5, no. 412 (May 1995). Review.
2. *Necrofile: The Review of Horror Fiction* (Summer 1995): 24+.
3. Ridge, Putney Tyson, Ph.D., (pseudonym for Straub). *"Ghosts:* Edited by Peter Straub—Remarks of a Concerned and Caring Friend." Online: http://net-site.com/straub/put_Gho.htm.
4. *Science Fiction Chronicle* Vol. 16 (August 1995): 49.

The Horror Writers Association Presents

PETER STRAUB'S

GHOSTS

What you can't
see can scare
you to death...

POCKET
STAR
BOOKS

Edited by Peter Straub

GHOSTS. New York, London: Pocket Star Books, April 1995.

THE HELLFIRE CLUB. New York: Random House, January 1996.

A21.
The Hellfire Club
(1996)

A21. *THE HELLFIRE CLUB.* New York: Random House, January 1996, 463 pp., $25.95, hardcover, 85,000 copies. ISBN 0-679-40137-7. LC 95-21773. Novel.

b. New York: Book-of-the-Month Club/Quality Paperback Book Club, February 1997, 463 pp., $12.95, trade paperback. Book Club Edition—Main Selection. No ISBN listed.

c. London: HarperCollins UK, July 1996, 463 pp., £15.99, hardcover. First British Edition. ISBN 0-00-225454-9.

d. Rockland MA: Wheeler, WHEELER LARGE PRINT BOOK SERIES, July 1996, xii+769 pp., $25.95, hardcover. ISBN 1-56895-337-2.

e. As: *De Hellfire Club.* Amsterdam, Netherlands: Luitingh-Sijthoff, 1996, 557 pp., fl 45,-/900 F, paperback. Dutch translation by Frank Visser. ISBN 902452458x.

f. As: *Hellfire Club.* Oslo, Norway: Aventura, 1996, 575 pp., hardcover. Norwegian translation by Tore Aurstad. ISBN 82-588-1224-6.

g. London: HarperCollins UK, June 1997, 588 pp., £5.99, paperback. Cover art by Michael Tevillion. ISBN 0-00-649848-5.

h. New York: Ballantine, March 1997, 526 pp., $6.99, mass-market paperback. International Edition.

i. New York: Ballantine, August 1997, 526 pp., $6.99, mass-market paperback. Domestic edition. ISBN 0-345-41500-0. 4th printing by 1999.

j. As: *Clube do Fogo do Inferno* ['Club of the Fire of Hell']. São Paulo, Brazil: Bertrand Brasil/BCD União de Editoras S.A, 1997, 602 pp., R$44,00. Portuguese translation by Luiza Ibañez. ISBN BKNET0000576436.

k. As: *Hellfire Club: Reise in die Nacht* ['Journey into the Night']. München, Germany: Wilhelm Heyne Verlag,1997, DM 48,00; hardcover. German translation by Joachim Körber. ISBN 3-453-12339-5.

l. As: *Le Club de l'enfer* ['The Club of Hell']. Paris, France: Editions Plon, April 1998, 491 pp., 139.00 FF, hardcover. French translation by Michel Pagel. Illustrated by Philippe Sohiez. Graphics by Didier Thimonier. ISBN 2-259-18431-6.

m. As: *Hellfire Club: Reise in die Nacht* ['Journey into the Night']. München, Germany: Wilhelm Heyne Verlag, HEYNE ALLGEMEINE REIHE #10585, September 1998, DM 16,90; paperback. German translation by Joachim Körber. ISBN 3-453-13649-7.

n. As*: Circulo Diabolico* ['Diabolic Circle']. 2nd edition. Barcelona, Spain: Editorial Planeta, S.A., PLANET DEXTER, June 1997, 560 pp., 3077 pta, hardcover. Spanish translation by Enric Tremps. ISBN 84-08-02053-6. Also issued as*: Circulo Diabolico*, Barcelona, Spain: Editorial Planeta, S.A., PLANET DEXTER, May 1998, 557 pp., $29.95, hardcover. ISBN 84-08-02053-6.

o. As: *O Clube de Fogo do Inferno* ['The Club of the Fire of Hell']. Rio de Janeiro, Brazil: Bertrand Brasill BCD Uniao de Editoras S. A., 1997, 598 pp., paperback. Portuguese translation by Luiza Ibanez. ISBN 85-286-0610-4.

p. As*: Circulo Diabolico* ['Diabolic Circle']. Barcelona, Spain: Editorial Planeta, S.A., PLANET DEXTER, April 1998, 560 pp., 1298 pta, paperback, Spanish translation by Enric Tremps. ISBN 84-08-02524-4.

q. As: *Le club de l'enfer* ['The Club of Hell']. Paris, France: Editions Pocket, TERREUR No. 9220, September 1999, 491 pp., [?] FF, paperback. French translation by Michel Pagel. Illustration by Pierre-Olivier Templier.

r. As audiotape: Simon & Schuster Audio, March 1996, $25.00, 4 cassettes. Read by Margaret Colin. ISBN 0671738607.

COMMENTS: The first edition states "First Edition" on the copyright page, with the number sequence 23456789.

SELECTED ARTICLES AND REVIEWS:
1. Bryant, Edward. *"The Hellfire Club*: Peter Straub." *Locus*, vol. 36, No. 422 (March 1996).
2. Chandler, Stacy Brown. *Library Journal* Vol. 120 (15 November 1995): 101. "Horror meets horror in this bizarre, enigmatic tale, which reveals itself in onion-like layers."
3. DeHaven, Tom. "Magical Mystery Tour." *Entertainment Weekly.* (9 February 1996): 46+ (2-pages).

4. Dunn, Katherine. *Washington Post.* 11 February 1996. Also Online: http://net-site.com/straub/dunn.htm. "As in Straub's previous big books, this is a gargantuan engine with multiple, meshing plots in which the sins of the past power the active evil of the present."

5. Guran, Paula. Review. *DarkEcho Horror.* Review Archive #3. Available online at: http://www.darkecho.com/darkecho/reviews/archrev3.html#hellfire. "Straub, a writer who has constantly challenged himself over the years, delights us this time with a sly switchblade hidden up the benign tweed sleeve of his traditional mainstream jacket."

6. Harrison, Colin. *The New York Times Book Review.* 25 February 1996: VIII, 9.

7. Hoffert, Barbara, and Mark Annichiario. "Prepub Alerts." *Library Journal* Vol. 120 (1 October 1995): 62.

8. *Infinitas: Science Fiction & Fantasy Bookshop* (Parammatta, NSW, Australia) Vol. 4, No. 6 (June 1997). Review; Available at: http://www.fandom.net/Infinitas/Newsletter/.

9. Kadet, Gary. "Formula Fatalities." *The Boston Book Review* 1 May 1996. Available at: http://www.bookwire.com/BBR/Fiction-&-Criticism2/read.Review$2467.

10. Kenney, Peter. *The Armchair Detective* Vol. 29 (Summer 1996): 376. "There are many different strands to the book.... Peter Straub is able to weave these pieces together with extraordinary skill and the result is a story which is riveting."

11. Lehmann-Haupt, Christopher. "Enough Fearful Twists for Everyone." *The New York Times* 1 February 1996: C, 17.

12. MacCulloch, Simon. "Vague but Nasty Secrets." *Necrofile: The Review of Horror Fiction* Issue 20 (Spring 1996). Online: http://net-site.com/straub/necrofil.htm. "The Hellfire Club substitutes for the relatively easy to grasp (and fight) figure of the vampire the whole fabric of gothic melodrama, whose ultimate implication is that reality is constantly on the verge of being lost entirely to someone's evil dream. In so doing, it confirms the value of Straub's more explicit and elaborate deployment of his chosen literary mode."

13. *Publishers Weekly* Vol. 244 (23 June 1997): 88. "Reprint Fiction" note.

14. Ridge, Putney Tyson, Ph.D. (pseudonym for Straub). *"The Hellfire Club."* Online: http://net-site.com/straub/pt_thc.htm.

15. Steinberg, Sybil S. "PW Forecasts: Fiction." *Publishers Weekly* Vol. 242 (27 November 1995): 49-50.

16. Walton, David. "Sure as Hellfire, Straub's Latest is intricate and

Bloody." *The Detroit News* 7 February 1996. Available at: http://www.detnews.com/menu/stories/34949.htm. "Straub's sure-to-be-a-best-seller is anything but tame, and aficionados will enjoy its intricacy, its many well-defined minor characters and the way the 'Night Journey' story frames Nora's life-and-death struggle."

17. Wilkinson, Joanne. Review. *Booklist* Vol. 92 (1 November 1995): 435.

Peter and PTR:

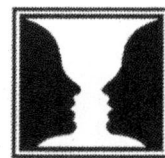

*Two Deleted Prefaces
and
an Introduction*

Peter Straub

PETER AND PTR: TWO DELETED PREFACES AND AN INTRODUCTION.
Subterranean Press, February 1999.

A22.

Peter and Ptr *(1999)*

A22. *PETER AND PTR: TWO DELETED PREFACES AND AN INTRODUCTION.*
Edited by Bill Shafer. Burton MI: Subterranean Press, February
1999, 31 pp., $40.00, hardcover; edition of 52 signed and lettered
copies. Deleted materials from *Mr. X.*
   b. Burton MI: Subterranean Press, February 1999, 31 pp., $10.00,
      chapbook; edition of 250 signed and numbered copies. No
      ISBN assigned.
   c. Burton MI: Subterranean Press, February 1999, 341 pp. A
      small number of copies with "Ptr" on the title page instead of
      "PTR."

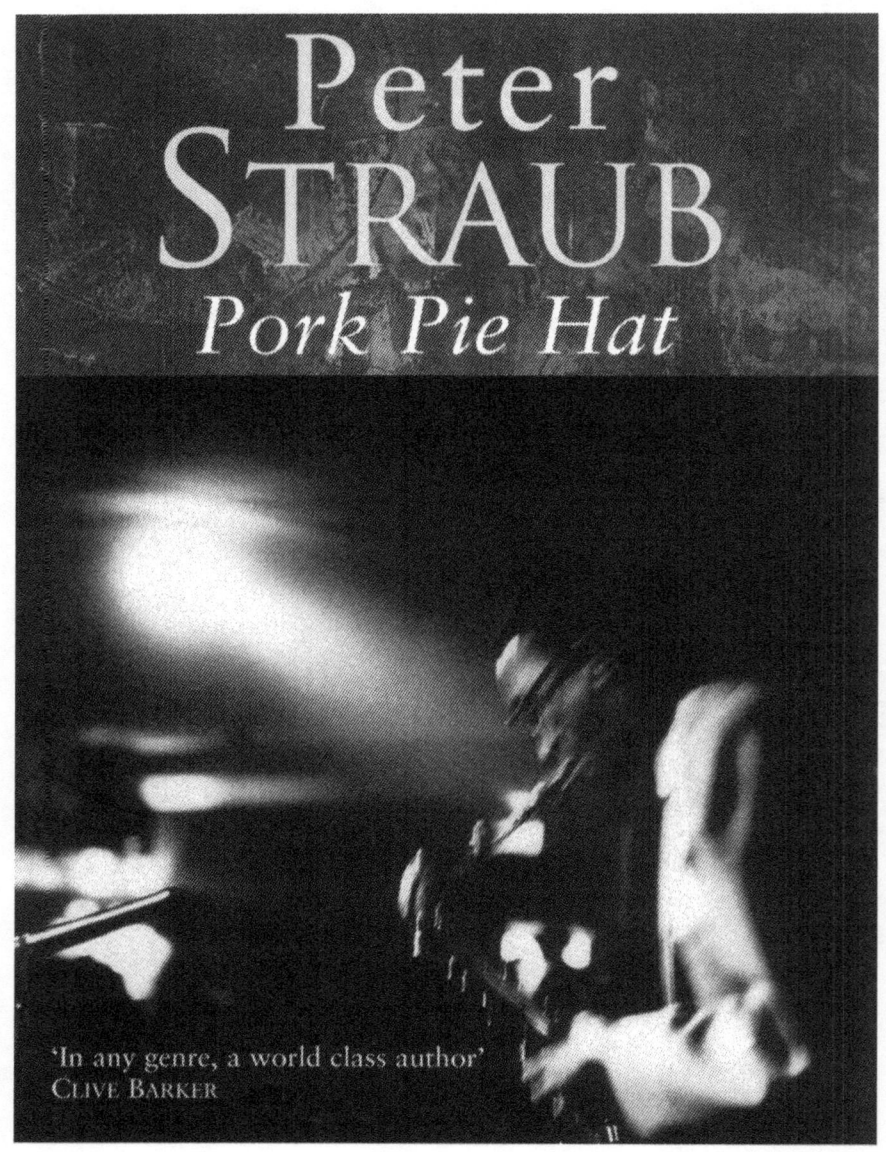

Peter
STRAUB

Pork Pie Hat

'In any genre, a world class author'
CLIVE BARKER

PORK PIE HAT. England: Orion (UK).

A23.

Pork Pie Hat *(1999)*

A23. *PORK PIE HAT.* England: Orion (UK), Criminal Record Series, July
1999, £6.99. ISBN 0-75282-512-7. [See A25, B21]

MR. X. New York: Random House, August 1999.

A24.

Mr. X *(1999)*

A24. *MR. X.* New York: Random House, August 1999, 483 pp., $25.95, 75,000 hardcover copies. ISBN 0679401385. LC number 98-47688. Novel.

  b. Paris, France: Editions Plon, 1999/2000, hardcover. French translation.

A25.

Magic Terror (2000)

A25. *MAGIC TERROR.* New York: Random House, 2000. Collection—
Short fiction.

    b. Magic Terror. England. The collection has not yet been placed
with an British publisher; it will include all of the stories listed
except "Pork Pie Hat" [see A23 above].

CONTENTS: "Ashputtle" [B19]; "Isn't It Romantic?" [B25]; "The
Ghost Village" [B18]; "Bunny is Good Bread" (formerly
"Fee")[B20]; "Pork Pie Hat" [A23, B21]; "Hunger: An
Introduction" [B22]; "Mr Clubb and Mr. Cuff" [B24]

B.
SHORT FICTION—
SHORT STORIES & NOVELLAS

1981

B1. "**THE GENERAL'S WIFE.**" *Twilight Zone Magazine* (May 1982). Novella. [See A10]

    b. The General's Wife. West Kingston RI: Donald M. Grant, 1982, 128 pp., hardcover, signed and numbered, 1200 copies. ISBN 0-937986-54-2. Illustrated by Tom Canty; introduction by Straub [See A10, C2].

1986

B2. "**ROUTINE TEUTON.**" *Bred Any Good Rooks Lately?* Edited by James Charlton. Garden City NY: Doubleday, 1986, 117 pp., $4.95, paperback. 83. ISBN 0-385-23477-5. Short-short story.

    b. Rpt. in: *Bred Any Good Rooks Lately? A Collection of Puns, Shaggy Dogs, Spoonerisms, Feghoots & Malappropriate Stories.* Gathered by James Charlton. Illustrated by Mary Kornblum. New York: Pennyfarthing/Dorset (division of Marboro Books), 1989, 117 pp., paperback. 83. ISBN 0-88029-411-6.

1988

B3. "**THE JUNIPER TREE.**" *Prime Evil: New Stories by the Masters of Modern Horror.* Edited by Douglas E. Winter. New York: NAL/Signet. June 1988, 322 pp., $18.95, hardcover. 181-214. ISBN 0-453-00572-1. Short story.

    b. In: *Prime Evil: New Stories by the Masters of Modern Horror.* Edited by Douglas Winter. West Kingston/Hampton Falls: Donald M. Grant, 1988, hardcover; limited edition of 1000 copies signed by Winter, Tom Canty (illustrator and designer) and contributors. Edited by Douglas E. Winter.

    c. In: *Prime Evil.* Edited by Douglas E. Winter. London: Bantam, 1988, 322 p., 11.95p, hardcover. 181-211. ISBN 0593-015-428.

    d. In: *Prime Evil.* Edited by Douglas E. Winter. London: Bantam, 1988, 352 pp., hardcover edition of 250 signed copies, leatherbound with turtle shell. 203-232. Illustrated First Edition. ISBN 0-937986-84-8.

e. In: *Prime Evil: New Stories by the Masters of Modern Horror.* New York: Signet, April 1989, 380 pp., $6.99,. mass-market paperback. 213-248. ISBN 0451159098.

f. Rpt. in: *Houses without Doors.* New York: Dutton, 1990. 59-90. [See A16].

g. As: "Le Genévrier." In *Trieze histoires diaboliques* [*Prime Evil*; 'Thirteen Diabolical Stories']. Edited by Douglas Winter. Paris, France: Albin Michel, November 1990, 410 pp., 130.00 FF/19.82 Euro, paperback. 233-270. French translation by Jean-Daniel Brèque. ISBN 2226049525

h. As: "Le Genévrier." In *13 histoires diaboliques* [*Prime Evil*]. Edited by Douglas E. Winter. Paris, France: Editions Presses Pocket, TERREUR #9074, November 1992, 44.00 FF, paperback. 267-310. French translation by Jean-Daniel Brèque. Illustrated by Pierre-Olivier Templier. ISBN 2-226-04722-1.

i. As: "Le Genévrier." In *Trieze histoires diaboliques* [*Prime Evil*]. Edited by Douglas Winter. Paris, France: De La Seine, August 1995, 76.00 FF/11.59 Euro. French translation. ISBN 273820841X.

j. Rpt. in: *The Armless Maiden.* Edited by Terri Windling. New York: Tor, April 1995, 382 pp., $22.95, hardcover. 96-119. ISBN 0-312-85234-7.

k. As audiotape: Included on *Prime Evil, Secrets and Shadows*, by Simon & Schuster Audio, 1990, 2 cassettes. Read by James B. Sikking.

COMMENTS: Contributors and stories included in *Prime Evil*: Clive Barker, "Coming to Grief"; Jack Cady, "By Reason of Darkness"; Ramsey Campbell, "Next Time You'll Know Me"; Dennis Etchison, "The Blood Kiss"; Charles L. Grant, "Spinning Tales with the Dead"; M. John Harrison, "The Great God Pan"; Paul Hazel, "Having a Woman at Lunch"; Stephen King, "The Night Flier"; Thomas Ligotti, "Alice's Last Adventure"; David Morrell, "Orange is for Anguish, Blue for Insanity"; Straub; Whitley Strieber, "The Pool"; and Thomas Tessier, "Food"

1989

B4. "FROM MRS. GOD." *Conjunctions: 14.* Edited by Bradford Morrow.

New York: Collier Books/Macmillan, December 1989, 285 pp., $9.95, trade paper. 84-97. ISBN 0-02-035290-5. Excerpt from *Mrs. God* [See A16, A17, B12]

1990

B5. "BLUE ROSE." *Houses without Doors*. New York: Dutton, 1990. 3-55. Novella [See A14, A16]

B6. "THE BUFFALO HUNTER." *Houses without Doors*. New York: Dutton, 1990. 109-207. Novella [See A16]

B7. "INTERLUDE: BAR TALK." *Houses without Doors*. New York: Dutton, 1990. 209-211. Short-short story/link [See A16]

B8. "INTERLUDE: GOING HOME." *Houses without Doors*. New York: Dutton, 1990. 91-92. Short-short story/link [See A16]

B9. "INTERLUDE: IN THE REALM OF DREAMS." *Houses without Doors*. New York: Dutton, 1990. 57. Short-short story/link [See A16]

B10. "INTERLUDE: THE POETRY READING." *Houses without Doors*. New York: Dutton, 1990. 107-108. Short-short story/link [See A16]

B11. "INTERLUDE: THE VETERAN." *Houses without Doors*. New York: Dutton, 1990. 221-222. Short-short story/link [See A16]

B12. "MRS. GOD" *Houses without Doors*. New York: Dutton, 1990. 223-352. Novella [See A16, A17, B4]

B13. "SHE SAW A YOUNG MAN." *Houses without Doors*. New York: Dutton, 1990. 1. Short-short story/link [See A16]

B14. "A SHORT GUIDE TO THE CITY." *Houses without Doors*. New York: Dutton, 1990. 93-105. Short story [See A16]
    b. Rpt in: *Iniquities* 1, no. 2 (Spring 1991): 48-55. Edited by Buddy Martinez. Pasadena CA: Iniquities Publications, 96 pp., $4.95, paperback. Cover art by J. K. Potter.
    c. Rpt in: *The Year's Best Fantasy and Horror: Fourth Annual Collections*. Edited by Ellen Datlow and Terri Windling. New

York: St. Martin's, July 1991, 552 pp., $15.95, trade paperback. 454-462. ISBN 0-312-06007-6.

d. Rpt in: *The Year's Best Fantasy and Horror: Fourth Annual Collections.* Edited by Ellen Datlow and Terri Windling. New York: St. Martin's, 1991, $27.95, hardcover. ISBN 0-312-06005-X.

e. Rpt in: *Best New Horror 2.* Edited by Stephen Jones and Ramsey Campbell. London [?]: Robinson, August 1991, 433 pp., £7.99, trade paper. 12-33. Cover art by Luis Rey. ISBN 1-85487-094-7.

f. Rpt in: *Best New Horror 2.* Edited by Stephen Jones and Ramsey Campbell. New York: Carroll & Graf, 1991. ISBN 0-88184-921-9

g. Rpt in: *The Giant Book of Best New Horror.* Edited by Stephen Jones and Ramsey Campbell. London [?]: Magpie, May 1993, xv+619 pp., £10.95, trade paperback. 73-84. ISBN 1-85487-193-5.

h. Rpt in: *American Gothic Tales.* Edited by Joyce Carol Oates. New York: Penguin/Plume, December 1996, 547 pp., $14.95, trade paperback. 358-368. ISBN 0-452-27489-3.

B15. "SOMETHING ABOUT A DEATH, SOMETHING ABOUT A FIRE." *Houses without Doors.* New York: Dutton, 1990. 213-219. Short story. [See A16]

b. Rpt. in: *Omni* 13, no 1 (October 1990): 90+.

B16. "THEN ONE DAY SHE SAW HIM AGAIN." *Houses without Doors.* New York: Dutton, 1990. 255-256. Short-short story link. [See A16]

1991

B17. "THE KINGDOM OF HEAVEN." *The New Gothic: A Collection of Contemporary Gothic Fiction.* Edited by Bradford Morrow and Patrick McGrath. New York: Random House, October 1991, 336 pp., $22.00, hardcover. 249-266. ISBN 0-394-58767-7. Short story; excerpted from *The Throat.*[see A19]

ANTHOLOGY REPRINTS:

b. New York: Book-of-the-Month-Club/Quality Paperback Guild.

c. New York: Vintage, October 1992, $13.00, trade paperback. ISBN 0-679-730-75-3.

d. New York: Vintage, 1994, paperback.

e. As: *the Picador Book of the New Gothic*. London: Picador, 1992, hardcover.

f. As: [German title unknown]. Frankfurt, Germany: S. Fischer Verlag, 1993. German translation.

g. As: [Spanish title unknown]. Barcelona, Spain: Edicione Minotauro, 1993. Spanish translation.

h. As: [Japanese title unknown]. 2 vols. Tokyo, Japan: Fukutake Shoten, 1993. Japanese translation.

i. London: Pan, 1994, paperback.

j. As: "Il Regno dei Cieli." *New Gothic. 21 Storie dell'ombra*. Milano [Milan], Italy: Arnoldo Mondadori Editore, 1996. 306-328. Italian translation by Massimo Bocchiola.

COMMENTS: Other authors included with Straub in the anthology—Bradford Morrow, Patrick McGrath, Martin Amis, Angela Carter, Emma Tennant, Ruth Rendell, John Edgar Wideman, Kathy Acker, William T. Vollmann, Joyce Carol Oates, Robert Coover, Lynne Tillman, Jamaica Kincaid, Jeanette Winterson, Paul West, Anne Rice, Yannick Murphy, Janice Galloway, Scott Bradfield, and John Hawkes.

SELECTED ARTICLES AND REVIEWS:
1. Winnett, Scott. Review of *The New Gothic. Locus* Vol. 28, No. 1, Issue 372 (January 1992).
2. Wolfe, Gene. Review of The New Gothic: A Collection of Contemporary Gothic Fiction. New York Review of Science Fiction #41 (January 1992): 1.

1992

B18. "THE GHOST VILLAGE." *MetaHorror*. Edited by Dennis Etchison. New York: Dell Abyss, July 1992, xvii+377 pp., $4.99, paperback. 334-377. ISBN 0-440-20899-8. Novella.

b. Rpt. in: *MetaHorror*. Edited by Dennis Etchison. West Kingston RI: Donald M. Grant, 1992, 318 pp., slipcased and illustrated hardcover, signed and numbered, 1000 copies. ISBN 1-880418-02-9.

    c. Rpt. In: *The Year's Best Fantasy and Horror: Sixth Annual Collection.* Edited by Ellen Datlow and Terri Windling. New York: St. Martin's, August 1993, 529 pp., $16.95, trade paperback. 497-58. ISBN 0-312-09422-1. [Hardcover edition announced, $27.95; ISBN 0-312-09421-1]

    d. Rpt. in: *The Mists from Beyond.* Edited by Robert Weinberg, Stefan R. Dziemianowicz, and Martin H. Greenberg. New York: Penguin/Roc, September 1993, 350 pp., $20.00, hardcover. 319+. ISBN 0-451-45239-9.

    e. Rpt. in: *Best New Horror 4.* Edited by Stephen Jones and Ramsey Campbell. New York: Carroll & Graf, November 1993, 413 pp., $21.95, hardcover. ISBN 0-7867-0004-1.

    f. Rpt. in: *Best New Horror 4.* Edited by Stephen Jones and Ramsey Campbell. London: Robinson, November 1993, hardcover. 375-403. Published simultaneously with the above title.

    g. Rpt. in: *The Giant Book of Terror.* Edited by Stephen Jones and Ramsey Campbell. England: Magpie, August 1994, 557 pp., £3.99, hardcover. 525-557. ISBN 1-85487-376-8.

    h. Rpt. in: *The Mists from Beyond.* Edited by Robert Weinberg, Stefan R. Dziemianowicz, and Martin H. Greenberg. New York: Penguin, 1995, 362 pp., &5.99, mass-market paperback. 330-362. ISBN 0-451-45498-7.

    i. Rpt. in: *New Masterpieces of Horror.* Edited by John Betancourt. New York: Barnes & Noble, September 1996, 514 pp., $7.98, hardcover. 367-400. ISBN 1-56619-790-2.

    j. Rpt. in: *The Giant Book of Terror.* Edited by Stephen Jones and Ramsey Campbell. Bristol: Parragon, 19__, £2.99, paperback. ISBN 0-7575-0142-9.

    k. Rpt. in: *Best New Horror.* Edited by Stephen Jones and Ramsey Campbell. London: Robinson, 19__, 481 pp., £6.99, paperback. 438-469. ISBN 1-85487-182-X.

    l. Rpt. in: *Horror Il Meglio* ['The Better Horror']. Edited by Stephen Jones and Ramsey Campbell. Milano, Italy: 19__, 468 pp., paperback. 436-468. Italian translation by Tullio Dobner. ISBN 88-429-0800-2.

    m. Rpt. in: *Magic Terror.* New York: Random House, 2000. [See A25]

COMMENTS: "The Ghost Village" acclaimed as Best Novella, World Fantasy Awards, 1993.

1994

B19. "ASHPUTTLE." *Black Thorn, White Rose.* Edited by Ellen Datlow and Terri Windling. New York: AvoNova/Morrow, September [August] 1994, 386 pp., $22.00. 281-305. ISBN 0-688-13713-X. Novella.

    b. Magic Terror. New York: Random House, 2000. [See A25].

B20. "FEE." *Borderlands 4.* Edited by Thomas F Monteleone. Grantham NH: Borderlands Press, November 1994. 330 pp., $65.00, hardcover, limited edition signed and numbered, 500 copies. No ISBN assigned.

    b. Borderlands 4. Edited by Thomas F. Monteleone. Clarkston GA: White Wolf Publishing (Borealis Imprint Logo), August 1995, 337 pp., $5.99, paperback. ISBN 1565041100.

    c. Rpt. in: *Dark Terrors.* Edited by Stephen Jones and David Sutton. London: Gollancz, October 1995, 379 pp., £15.99, hardcover anthology. 316-379. ISBN 0-575-06136-7.

    d. Rpt. in: *Dark Terrors.* Edited by Stephen Jones and David Sutton. London: Vista, 19__, 379 pp., £5.99, mass-market paperback. 316-379. ISBN 0-575-60024-1.

    e. As: "Bunny is Good Bread." *Magic Terror.* New York: Random House, 2000. [See A25]

B21. "PORK PIE HAT." *Murder for Halloween: Tales of Suspense.* Edited by Michele Slung and Roland Hartman. New York: Mysterious Press, 1994, 362 pp., hardcover. Novella. [See A23, A25]

    b. Rpt. in *The Armchair Detective* Vol. 27, No. 4 (Fall 1994): 440-467.

    c. *Murder for Halloween: Tales of Suspense.* Edited by Michele Slung and Roland Hartman. New York: Warner Books, 1995, 412 pp., $5.99, mass-market paperback. 339-412. ISBN 0-446-40461-6.

    d. Rpt. in *The Year's 25 Best Mystery Stories.* 1997.

    e. Online: http://net-site.com/straub/pork.htm.

    f. Rpt in: *Polar* No. 19 (1998): 86-153. French translation by Jean-Paul Gratias.

1995

B22. "HUNGER: AN INTRODUCTION." *Peter Straub's Ghosts*. Edited by Peter Straub. New York, London: Pocket Star, 1995. 1-41. Novella. [See A20]

    b. Rpt. in: *Dark Terror 2*. Edited by Stephen Jones and David Sutton. London: Gollancz, October 1996, 379 pp., £16.99, hardcover. 341-379. ISBN 0-575-06326-2.

    c. Rpt. in: *Magic Terror.* New York: Random House, 2000. [See A25]

B23. "IN TRANSIT," by Peter Straub and Benjamin Straub. *Great Writers and Their Kids Write Spooky Stories*. Edited by Martin Greenberg, Jill M. Morgan, and Robert Weinberg. New York: Random House, October 1995, 224 pp., $16.00. 123-150. Short story.

1997

B24. "MR. CLUBB AND MR. CUFF." *Murder for Revenge*. Edited by Otto Penzler. New York: Avon, 1997. Novella. Anthology of twelve original stories by Straub, Lawrence Block, Mary Higgins Clark, Thomas Cook, Vicki Hendricks, Joan Hess, Judith Kelman, Eric Lustbader, Phillip Margolin, David Morrell, Joyce Carol Oates, and Shel Silverstein.

    b. Rpt in: *Murder For Revenge*. Edited by Otto Penzler. New York: Delacorte, April 1998, $21.95, hardcover. ISBN 0-385-31715-8.

    c. As: "Radical Disjunctures: An Excerpt from Mr. Clubb and Mr. Cuff." *Dark Carnival Bookstore*. Available at: http://www.darkcarnival.com/DCOLarchive/straub0.htm.

    d. Rpt. in: *Legacies*. Edited by Richard Chizmar. Abingdon MD: Cemetery Dance Publications, February 1999, $200.00(?), signed, limited edition. Anthology of ten reprinted stories by Straub, Dean R. Koontz, Clive Barker, Ray Bradbury, and others.

    e. Online: http://net-site.com/straub/clubb.htm.

    f. As: "Mr Clubb et Mr Cuff." *Vengeances mortelles* (*Murder for Revenge*). Edited by Otto Penzler. Paris, France: Editions Albin

Michel, February 1999, 130.00 FF, hardcover. 325-457. French translation by Anne Damour and William Olivier Desmond. ISBN 2-226-10519-0.

g. Rpt. in: *Murder for Revenge.* Edited by Otto Penzler. New York: Dell/Random House, March 1999, 388 pp., $5.99, trade paperback. 281-388. ISBN 0-440-22321-0.

h. Rpt. in: *Magic Terror.* New York: Random House, 2000. [See A25]

COMMENTS: Nominated for the 1998 World Horror Awards, Best Long Form.

1998

B25. "ISN'T IT ROMANTIC?" *Murder on the Run.* By The Adams Round Table. February 1998, 336, $21.99, hardcover. 217-268. ISBN 0425161463. Short story.

    b. Online at: http://net-site.com/straub/romance.htm.

    c. Rpt in: *Magic Terror.* New York: Random House, 2000. [See A25]

    d. As audiocassette: *Murder on the Run.* Durkin Hayes, August 1998, $29.95. Abridged. Read by Eric Conger. ISBN 0886464706.

SELECTED ARTICLES AND REVIEWS:
1. *Booklist* February 15, 1988.
2. Klett, Rex. *Library Journal.* Vol. 123, No. 2 (1 February 1998): 116.
3. *Kirkus Reviews* January 1, 1998.

1999

B26. [TITLE UNKNOWN]. *Dead Ends: Angloamerikanische Horrorgeschichten* ['Anglo-American Horror Stories']. __: Jens Neumann, 1999, 200 pp., dm 32,-, paperback. German translations by Frank Vesta and Jens Schumacher. ISBN 3-930559-67-6. [This item has been reported but not yet verified.]

C.
Non–Fiction–
Introductions, Essays,
Reviews & Afterwords

1982

C1. "MEETING STEVIE." *Fear Itself: The Horror Fiction of Stephen King.* Edited by Tim Underwood and Chuck Miller. San Francisco CA: Underwood-Miller, 1982. Hardcover, signed, numbered edition of 225 copies signed by Straub, Stephen King, Fritz Lieber, Charles L. Grant, Alan Ryan, Douglas E. Winter, Ben P. Indick, Deborah Notkin, Don Herron, Bill Warren, Chelsea Quinn Yarboro). Introduction.

    b. "Meeting Stevie." *Fear Itself: The Horror Fiction of Stephen King.* Edited by Tim Underwood and Chuck Miller. San Francisco CA: Underwood-Miller, 1982, hardcover, trade edition, 4775 copies.

    c. "Meeting Stevie." *Fear Itself: The Horror Fiction of Stephen King.* Edited by Tim Underwood and Chuck Miller. New York: Plume/NAL, June 1984, 277 pp., $7.95, trade paperback. 7-14. ISBN 0452006848.

C2. "INTRODUCTION." *THE GENERAL'S WIFE.* West Kingston RI: Donald M. Grant, November 1982, 128 pp., hardcover. ISBN 0937986542. [See also A10, B1]

1983

C3. "INTRODUCTION." *In a Lonely Place.* Karl Edward Wagner. New York: Warner Books, March 1983, 265 pp. Paperback.

    b. Santa Cruz CA: Scream Press, December 1984, 249 pp., $35.00, hardcover limited signed, numbered, and boxed edition; $15.00 trade edition. xv+. ISBN 0-910489-4.

1988

C4. "INTRODUCTION." *The Wine-Dark Sea.* Robert Aickman. New York: Arbor House/William Morrow, October 1988, 388 pp., hardcover. 7-10. ISBN 1-55710-035-7. Eleven stories, with introduction by Straub.

b. [London?]: Mandarin, March 1990, 352 pp., £3.99, paperback. 7-10. ISBN 0-7493-0172-4. This collection includes only eight of the original eleven stories.

C5. "STEPHEN KING: *THE SHINING.*" *Horror: 100 Best Books.* Edited by Stephen Jones and Kim Newman. Foreword by Ramsey Campbell. London: Xanadu Publications, 1988, 256 pp., hardcover. Limited signed edition of 300 copies.
b. London: Xanadu Publications, 1986, 256 pp., hardcover. Trade edition.
c. New York: Carroll & Graf, 1988, pp., hardcover.
d. "Stephen King: *The Shining.*" *Horror: 100 Best Books.* Edited by Stephen Jones and Kim Newman. Foreword by Ramsey Campbell. New York: Carroll & Graf, 1990, pp. 171-172. Trade paperback. Essay.
e. New York: Carroll & Graf, 1998. 10th anniversary edition of the collection.

1990

C6. "AUTHOR'S NOTE" *Houses without Doors.* 1990. Short story [See A16]

C7. "INTRODUCTION" to "Ringing the Changes," by Robert Aickman. *Dark Voices: The Best from the Pan Book of Horror Stories.* Edited by Stephen Jones and Clarence Paget. London: Pan, April 1990, 348 pp., £3.99, paperback. 191-192. Cover art by Dave McKean. ISBN 0-330-31100-X. Slipcased edition: ISBN 0330-31565-X.

C8. "MYSTERY, Mystery and Mystery Novels." *Mystery Scene Magazine* #24 (January 1990).

1992

C9. "ON MORTALITY AND CHANGE." Afterword to *Brief Lives,* by Neil Gaiman. *The Sandman 41-49.* New York: DC Comics, 1992-1993. Illustrated by Jill Thompson and Vince Locke.
b. As: "On Mortality and Change." Afterword to *Brief Lives,* by Neil Gaiman. *The Sandman, 41-49.* New York: DC Comics,

January 1995, 256 pp., $15.95, paperback. Illustrated by Jill Thompson and Vince Locke. ISBN: 1-56389-138-7. ISBN:1-56389-137-9 (hardcover)

C10. "THE FIFTIES." *Graven Images: The Best of Horror, Fantasy, and Science Fiction Film Art from the Collection of Ron Borst.* Edited by Ronald V. Borst, Keith Burns, and Leith Adams. Introduction by Stephen King. New York: Grove Press, 1992, xv+240 pp., $50.00. ISBN 0802114849. Reminiscence by Straub, Forrest J. Ackerman, Clive Barker, Robert Bloch, Ray Bradbury, and Harlan Ellison.

1993

C11. "INTRODUCTION." *Too Many Cooks*, by Rex Stout. New York: Bantam, September 1993, 237 pp.

1995

C12. "INTRODUCTION" to "The Cloak," by Robert Bloch. *Robert Bloch: Appreciations of the Master.* Edited by Richard Matheson and Ricia Mainhardt. New York: Tor, October 1995, 382 pp., $24.95, hardcover. 29-31. ISBN 0-312-85976-7.
   b. Robert Bloch: Appreciations of the Master. Edited by Richard Matheson and Ricia Mainhardt. New York: Tor, 19__, $16.95, trade paperback. ISBN 0312863583.

C13. "THE ONE, THE ONLY R. C., THEN, NOW, AND FOREVER." *The Core of Ramsey Campbell: A Bibliography and Reader's Guide.* Ramsey Campbell, with Stefan Dziemianowicz and S. T. Joshi. West Warwick RI: Necronomicon Press, 1995.
   b. Rpt. in: *Demons by Day Light.* Ramsey Campbell . 1998 [?]
   c. Rpt. in: *Dämonen bei Tag* ['Demons by Day']. __, Germany: Edition Metzengerstein, August 1998, 244 pp., DM 28,00; paperback. ISBN 3-932320-08-5

C14. "WILLIAM F. NOLAN: AN INTRODUCTION." *Night Shapes* by William F. Nolan. Baltimore MD: CD Publications, August 1995, 341 pp., $50.00, hardcover, signed (Straub and William F. Nolan), limited, slipcased edition, 500. 13-18. Illustrated by Alan M. Clark.

Afterword by Robert Bloch. ISBN 1-881475-14-X. Introduction to a volume of Nolan's short fiction.

1996

C15. [INTRODUCTION]. *The Island of Dr. Moreau,* by H. G. Wells. Photoplay Editions #279. New York: Modern Library, August 1996, 185 pp., $14.95, hardcover. 100th Anniversary Edition, issued to coincide with the release of the motion picture (starring Marlon Brando and Val Kilmer). Signed by director John Frankenheimer

1997

C16. "45 CALIBRATIONS OF RAYMOND CHANDLER. *Conjunctions* [Annandale-on-Hudson], 29 (Fall 1997). Article.
b. Rpt: http://www.conjunctions.com/archives/c29-ps.htm

C17. "VARIOUS ENCOUNTERS WITH KARL." *Exorcisms and Ecstasies.* Karl Edward Wagner. Minneapolis MN: Fedogan & Bremer, October 1997, 459 pp., $32.00, hardcover. 3-10. ISBN 1-878252-28-3. Appreciation/article in a collection of Wagner's fiction and poetry.
b. Limited edition. ISBN 1-878252-32-1.

1998

C18. "INTRODUCTION." *Are You Loathsome Tonight?* By Poppy Z. Brite. Springfield PA: Gauntlet books, 1998, 193 pp., $40.00. Collection of short fiction.

C19. COMMENTS FOR THE *PEOPLE* ONLINE CONFERENCE. 1998. Excerpts posted April 8 1998 at: http://www.horrornet.com/authors.htm. Straub discusses his plans for a second collection of short fiction, his responses to other horror writers, and his feelings about the future of the internet, and particularly of internet novels.

1999

C20. "BUNJEE JUMPING WITHOUT A CORD, PLUS SOME COMMENTS ON STYLE." *If: The Magazine of Speculative Fiction.* Writers Workshops (Brief Articles on the Craft by Established Authors.) Internet: March 3, 1999. At: http://www.natcom.org/if/.

C21. "THE FANTASY OF EVERYDAY LIFE" [Guest of Honor Address]. *Flashes of the Fantastic: Selected Essays from the War of the Worlds Centennial, Nineteenth International Conference on the Fantastic in the Arts.* New York: Greenwood Press, 1999 (?).

2000

C22. "LOOKING BACK." *Mothers & Sons.* Edited by Jill Morgan and Martin Greenberg. New York: Signet/Dutton, 2000.Essay/Memoir.

D.
POETRY

D1. "MY LIFE IN PICTURES." *My Life in Pictures*. Dublin: Seafront Press, 1971, 4 pp., 10 pence, stapled pamphlet. Poetry; 3 parts, [see A1]
  b. Rpt. in: *Leeson Park and Belsize Square: Poems 1970-1975*. San Francisco CA, Columbia PA: Underwood-Miller, October 1983, 20-22. [see A11]

  CONTENTS: 1. "Rescued by Rover"; 2. "How I Filmed Nanook"; 3. "Rushes, Goals"

D2. "THE DESERT MOTION." *Poetry* [Chicago IL].
  b. Rpt. in *Ishmael*. London: Turret Books, 1972. Free-verse stanzas, 14 lines. [see A2]
  c. Rpt in: *Leeson Park and Belsize Square: Poems 1970-1975*. San Francisco CA, Columbia PA: Underwood-Miller, October 1983, 30. [see A11]

D3. "THE BOW." *Poetry* [Chicago IL].
  b. Rpt. in: *Ishmael*. London: Turret Books, 1972. Free-verse stanzas, 9 lines, alternating couplets and single lines. [see A2]
  c. Rpt in: *Leeson Park and Belsize Square: Poems 1970-1975*. San Francisco CA, Columbia PA: Underwood-Miller, October 1983, 32. [see A11]

D4. "USING THE BOW." *Poetry* [Chicago IL].
  b. Rpt. in: *Ishmael*. London: Turret Books, 1972. Free-verse, 21 lines without stanza breaks. [see A2]
  c. Rpt in: *Leeson Park and Belsize Square: Poems 1970-1975*. San Francisco CA, Columbia PA: Underwood-Miller, October 1983, 30. [see A11]

D5. "THE SLEEPERS." *Poetry* [Chicago IL].
  b. Rpt. in: *Ishmael*. London: Turret Books, 1972. Stanzaic; 28 lines in 4-line shaped stanzas [see A2]
  c. Rpt in: *Leeson Park and Belsize Square: Poems 1970-1975*. San Francisco CA, Columbia PA: Underwood-Miller, October 1983, 37. [see A11]

D6. ON HAMPSTEAD HEATH WITH WOMEN." *Poetry* [Chicago IL].
  b. Ishmael. London: Turret Books, 1972. Stanzaic; 22 lines. [see A2]
  c. Rpt in: *Leeson Park and Belsize Square: Poems 1970-1975*. San

Francisco CA, Columbia PA: Underwood-Miller, October 1983, 41. [see A11]

D7. "THE FIRST BEDOUIN." *Ishmael.* London: Turret Books, 1972. Free-verse stanzas, 18 lines. [see A2]
    b. Rpt. in: *Leeson Park and Belsize Square: Poems 1970-1975*. San Francisco CA, Columbia PA: Underwood-Miller, October 1983, 29. [see A11]

D8. "ISHMAEL'S SONG TO HIS SISTER." *Ishmael.* London: Turret Books, 1972. Free-verse stanzas; 11 lines. [see A2]
    b. Rpt. in: *Leeson Park and Belsize Square: Poems 1970-1975*. San Francisco CA, Columbia PA: Underwood-Miller, October 1983, 31. [see A11]

D9. "ISHMAEL IN MANHATTAN." *Ishmael.* London: Turret Books, 1972. Free-verse; 10 lines in 5 couplets. [see A2]
    b. Rpt. in: *Leeson Park and Belsize Square: Poems 1970-1975*. San Francisco CA, Columbia PA: Underwood-Miller, October 1983, 34. [see A11]

D10. "DOWNTOWN, WAY DOWN." *Ishmael.* London: Turret Books, 1972. Free-verse; 4 triples, followed by a couplet and a single line. [see A2]
    b. Rpt. in: *Leeson Park and Belsize Square: Poems 1970-1975*. San Francisco CA, Columbia PA: Underwood-Miller, October 1983, 35. [see A11]

D11. "THE MUSIC HE HEARS." *Ishmael.* London: Turret Books, 1972. Free-verse; 4 stanzas, alternating triples and couplets. [see A2]
    b. Rpt. in: *Leeson Park and Belsize Square: Poems 1970-1975*. San Francisco CA, Columbia PA: Underwood-Miller, October 1983, 36. [see A11]

D12. "SONG FOR ONE ON WATER." *Ishmael.* London: Turret Books, 1972. Free-verse; two stanzas, 11 lines. [see A2]
    b. Rpt. in: *Leeson Park and Belsize Square: Poems 1970-1975*. San Francisco CA, Columbia PA: Underwood-Miller, October 1983, 38. [see A11]

D13. "A LOOSENING, A SPENDING PROSE." *Ishmael.* London: Turret

Books, 1972. Prose-poem. [see A2]

    b. Rpt. in: *Leeson Park and Belsize Square: Poems 1970-1975.* San Francisco CA, Columbia PA: Underwood-Miller, October 1983, 39. [see A11]

D14. "FROM LAWRENCE'S LETTERS: February 1915, Cornwall." *Ishmael.* London: Turret Books, 1972. Syllabics; 18 lines, most varying 9, 10, and 11 syllables. [see A2]

    b. Rpt. in: *Leeson Park and Belsize Square: Poems 1970-1975.* San Francisco CA, Columbia PA: Underwood-Miller, October 1983, 40. [see A11]

D15. "ENVOI FROM A BROTHER." *Ishmael.* London: Turret Books, 1972. Stanzaic; 12 lines in quartets. [see A2]

    c. Rpt. in: *Leeson Park and Belsize Square: Poems 1970-1975.* San Francisco CA, Columbia PA: Underwood-Miller, October 1983, 42. [see A11]

D16. "FOX SURVIVES." *Open Air.* Dublin: Irish University Press, 1972. 13. [see A3]

D17. "FOX IN SNOW." *Open Air.* Dublin: Irish University Press, 1972. 14. [see A3]

D18. "CIRCLING THE GROUND." *Open Air.* Dublin: Irish University Press, 1972. 15. [see A3]

D19. "TRACKING." *Open Air.* Dublin: Irish University Press, 1972. 16. [see A3]

D20. "FOX READING." *Open Air.* Dublin: Irish University Press, 1972. 17. [see A3]

D21. "FOX'S ADDRESS TO THE DELEGATES." *Open Air.* Dublin: Irish University Press, 1972. 18. [see A3]

D22. FOX'S ARROGANCE." *Open Air.* Dublin: Irish University Press, 1972. 19. [see A3]

D23. "FOX BY THE POOL." *Open Air.* Dublin: Irish University Press, 1972. 20-21. [see A3]

D24. "EXPLICATIONS." *Open Air.* Dublin: Irish University Press, 1972. 22. [see A3]

D25. "WOLF ON THE PLAINS." *Open Air.* Dublin: Irish University Press, 1972. 27. [see A3]

D26. "WORDS FROM THE ISLAND." *Open Air.* Dublin: Irish University Press, 1972. 28-29. [see A3]

D27. "MUHAMMED'S SONG." *Open Air.* Dublin: Irish University Press, 1972. 30. [see A3]

D28. "WOLF'S LITANY." *Open Air.* Dublin: Irish University Press, 1972. 31. [see A3]

D29. "WOLF AND THE TERRITORY." *Open Air.* Dublin: Irish University Press, 1972. 32-35. [see A3]

D30. "PREPARATIONS FOR DYING." *Open Air.* Dublin: Irish University Press, 1972. 36. [see A3]

D31. "ISOBEL'S RECITATIVE." *Open Air.* Dublin: Irish University Press, 1972. 37. [see A3]

D32. "AFTER THE RETURN." *Open Air.* Dublin: Irish University Press, 1972. 38. [see A3]

D33. "THE BLESSING." *Open Air.* Dublin: Irish University Press, 1972. 39. [see A3]

D34. "COMING TO ONE." *Open Air.* Dublin: Irish University Press, 1972. 40. [see A3]

D41. "ENCANTADAS." *Poetry.* Stanzaic; three parts, 13 alternating 5- and 6-line stanzas.
    b. Rpt in: *Leeson Park and Belsize Square: Poems 1970-1975.* San Francisco CA, Columbia PA: Underwood-Miller, October 1983, 23. [see A11]

D42. "MAKING THE CIRCLE'S FIGURE: FIVE FRENCH POEMS." *Atlantis.*
Free-verse.
  b. Rpt. in: *Leeson Park and Belsize Square: Poems 1970-1975.* San
    Francisco CA, Columbia PA: Underwood-Miller, October
    1983, 53-55. [see A11]

CONTENTS: 1. "In Whispers," after Jules Supervielle; 2. "'You,'"
after Robert Desnos; "Urn," after Jacques Dupin; 4. "The
Fatherland," after Yves Bonnefoy; 5. "Transfer," after André du
Bouchet.

D43. "'FACING THE LAVISH WEATHER.'" *The Massachusetts Review.* Free
verse; 3 stanzas, 26 lines.
  b. Rpt. in: *Leeson Park and Belsize Square: Poems 1970-1975.*
    San Francisco CA, Columbia PA: Underwood-Miller, October
    1983, 15. [see A11]

D44. "FACING LAND'S END." *The Massachusetts Review.* "For James
Tate"; 6 couplets/1 triplet, 15 lines.
  b. Rpt. in: *Leeson Park and Belsize Square: Poems 1970-1975.* San
    Francisco CA, Columbia PA: Underwood-Miller, October
    1983, 16. [see A11]

D45. "A TRIPLE-DECKER NOVEL." *The New Statesman.* Stanzaic; 18
lines in triplets, a quartet, and a couplet.
  b. Rpt. in: *Leeson Park and Belsize Square: Poems 1970-1975.* San
    Francisco CA, Columbia PA: Underwood-Miller, October
    1983, 40. [see A11]

D46. "THE FIGURES ON THE BEACH." *Leeson Park and Belsize Square:
Poems 1970-1975.* San Francisco CA, Columbia PA: Underwood-
Miller, October 1983, 17. Stanzaic, 7 5-line stanzas, quoting W. H.
Auden. [see A11]

D47. "READING THE WELL." *Leeson Park and Belsize Square: Poems
1970-1975.* San Francisco CA: Columbia PA: Underwood-Miller,
October 1983, 19. Single stanza, 15 couplets of alternating lengths.
[see A11]

D48. "FOR ANN LAUTERBACH." *Leeson Park and Belsize Square: Poems
1970-1975.* San Francisco CA: Columbia PA: Underwood-Miller,

October 1983, 46. Free-verse paragraphics, 26 lines. [see A11]

D49. **"FROM THE HEIAN COURT."** *Leeson Park and Belsize Square: Poems 1970-1975.* San Francisco CA: Columbia PA: Underwood-Miller, October 1983, 47. Stanzaic; 24 lines. [see A11]

D50. **"COMING TO REST."** *Leeson Park and Belsize Square: Poems 1970-1975.* San Francisco CA: Columbia PA: Underwood-Miller, October 1983, 48. 13 lines, broken into 26 alternating hemistiches.. [see A11]

D51. **"PHOTOGRAPHIC PLATE."** *Leeson Park and Belsize Square: Poems 1970-1975.* San Francisco CA: Columbia PA: Underwood-Miller, October 1983, 49. Four parts; 28 lines. [see A11]

D52. **"WITHSTANDING, SAVING, MOVING."** *Leeson Park and Belsize Square: Poems 1970-1975.* San Francisco CA: Columbia PA: Underwood-Miller, October 1983, 48. Three parts; 31 lines. [see A11]

CONTENTS: 1. "In Exile" after Frances Jammes; "Living In A Woman," after Henry Michaux; 3. "The Constructs," after St.-John Perce.

D53. **"LICHENS,"** after Jacques Dupin. *Leeson Park and Belsize Square: Poems 1970-1975.* San Francisco CA: Columbia PA: Underwood-Miller, October 1983, 56-58. Prose-poem in nine parts. [see A11]

D54. **"THE TRACE,"** for Anne Ricker. *Leeson Park and Belsize Square: Poems 1970-1975.* San Francisco CA: Columbia PA: Underwood-Miller, October 1983, 59-64. Free verse and prose poems in two parts, with 10 sub-parts. [see A11]

D55. **"LESSIVE."** *Leeson Park and Belsize Square: Poems 1970-1975.* San Francisco CA: Columbia PA: Underwood-Miller, October 1983, 67-68. Prose-poem. [see A11]

D56. **"SENTENCES FROM RIMBAUD."** *Leeson Park and Belsize Square: Poems 1970-1975.* San Francisco CA: Columbia PA: Underwood-Miller, October 1983, 69. Prose-poem. [see A11]

D57. **"FOR THOMAS TESSIER."** *Leeson Park and Belsize Square: Poems 1970-1975.* San Francisco CA: Columbia PA: Underwood-Miller,

October 1983, 70-71. Prose-poem in 3 block paragraphs. [see A11]

D58. **"Text,"** for Marcelin Pleynet. *Leeson Park and Belsize Square: Poems 1970-1975.* San Francisco CA: Columbia PA: Underwood-Miller, October 1983, 72-73. Free verse prose-poem. [see A11]

E.
LINER NOTES:
RECORDS & CDs

E1. *A SAILBOAT IN THE MOONLIGHT.* Ruby Braffa and Scott Hamilton. Concord CA: Concord Records, 1986. CJ 296.
   b. CD issue.

E2. *HEAVEN.* Phil Woods Quintet. Blackhawk Records BKH 50401-D, 1986.
   b. CD issue.

E3. *SOFT LIGHTS & SWEET MUSIC.* Scott Hamilton and Gerry Mulligan. Concord CA: Concord Records, 1986. CJ300.
   b. CD issue: CCD-4300.

E4. *DOUBLE EXPOSURE.* Ken Peplowski. Concord CA: Concord Records, 1987. CJ-344. Recorded, December 1987.
   b. CD issue: Concord CA: Concord Jazz, 1988, $17.49. CCD-4344. Five pages of program notes by Straub inserted into container.

E5. *EASY GOING.* Warren Vache Sextet. Concord CA: Concord Records, June 1987. CJ-323.
   b. CD issue: 1987, CCD-4323.

E6. *SHOW TUNES.* Rosemary Clooney. Concord Records CJ 364, 1988.
   b. CD issue __, 1988.

E7. *RADIO CITY.* Scott Hamilton Quintet. Concord CA: Concord Records CCCD 4428, 1990.

E8. *ALL BIRD'S CHILDREN.* Phil Woods Quintet. Concord Jazz, 1991, CCD-4441.

E9. *THE JON GORDON QUARTET.* Jon Gordon. New York: Chiaroscuro, 1992. CR (D) 316.

E10. [TITLE UNKNOWN]. Junior Mance. New York: Chiaroscuro, 1992. CR (D).

E11. *SCOTT HAMILTON WITH STRINGS.* Scott Hamilton. Concord CA: Concord Records CCD-4538, 1993.

E12. *INTO THE WOODS: THE BEST OF PHIL WOODS.* Phil Woods Quintet. Concord CA: Concord Jazz, April 1996, CCD-4699

E13. *JOE HELLENY: LIP SERVICE.* Arbors Records, CD, 1996.

E14. *TALK TO ME BABY.* Warren Vache. Muse MCD 5547, 1996.

E15. *AFTER HOURS.* Scott Hamilton. Concord CA: Concord Jazz, April 1997, CCD-4755-2.

E16. *THE SUNSET AND THE MOCKINGBIRD.* Tommy Flagan Trio. Blue Note Records. 1998.

F.
MISCELLANEOUS ITEMS

F1. *LORD JOHN SIGNATURES.* Anonymous Editor [Stephen King]. Northridge CA: Lord John Press, 1991, limited edition of 26 lettered copies. Introduction by Stephen King.

CONTENTS: Small-press collection of signed photographs, including Straub, John Barth, Robert Bloch, Ray Bradbury, Ramsey Campbell, Dennis Etchison, Tony Hillerman, Ursula K. Le Guin, Joyce Carol Oates, Dan Simmons, John Updike, Donald E. Westlake, and others.

F2. *THE FACES OF FANTASY.* Photographs by Patti Perret. New York: Tor Books, 19__, 235 pp., $22.95, hardcover. ISBN 0-312-86216-4.

F3. **1997 DARK PROGRESS, HORROR WRITERS CALENDAR.** Illustrated by Steve Montiglio.

COMMENTS: Writers include Straub, Edward Bryant, Leigh Clark, Douglas Clegg, Robert Devereaux, Yvonne Navarro, William F. Nolan, Matthew J. Pallamary, William Relling, Jr., David J. Schow and Christa Faust, Lucy Taylor, and Douglas E. Winter. Make a Wish Foundation.

F4. **INTERNATIONAL CONFERENCE ON THE FANTASTIC IN THE ARTS, 1998, GUEST OF HONOR.** March 18-21, 1998. Airport Hilton, Ft. Lauderdale FL.

F5. **PETER STRAUB AT THE ELECTRONIC POETRY CENTER.** 1999. Available at: http://wings.buffalo.edu/epc/.
CONTENTS: Two half-hour programs (30 minutes); three-minute selection of Straub reading from "Hunger" [see B22]; two minute 30 second selection of Straub reading from "Mr Clubb and Mr Cuff [see B24]; 2 minute 30 second selection of Straub reading from *The Throat* in RealAudio format.

F6. **WORLD HORROR 2000, GUEST OF HONOR.** Denver CO. May 11-14, 2000.

G.

Selected Secondary Sources:
Interviews, Reviews, Articles,
Biographical Sketches, Etc.

(Excluding in most cases Articles, Reviews, and Other
Studies Listed under Individual Works Above)

Alexander, David. Interview with Straub. *Samhain* #20 (April-May 1990). Two-page-interview; tie-in with the UK release of *Mystery*.

Barbato, Joseph. Interview with Straub. *Publishers Weekly* 28 January 1983: 39-40.

Barron, Neil, ed. *Horror Literature: A Reader's Guide.* New York: Garland, 1990. 178, 285-289, and others.

Bosky, Bernadette. "Stephen King and Peter Straub: Fear and Friendship." *Discovering Stephen King.* Edited by Darrell Schweitzer. STARMONT STUDIES IN LITERARY CRITICISM #8. Mercer Island, WA: Starmont House, 1985. 55-82. Simultaneous hardcover and paperback publication.

Brown, Charles N. "Peter Straub." *Locus* Vol. 24, No. 4, Issue 351 (April 1990). Interview.

Brown, Charles N. "Peter Straub." *Locus* Vol. 32, No. 1, Issue 396 (January 1994). Interview

Bryant, Ed. *Omni Visions.* June 5, 1997. Available online at: http://www.omnimag.com/archives/chats/ov060597.html. Interview.

Clute, John, and John Grant, eds. "Straub, Peter." *The Encyclopedia of Fantasy.* New York: St. Martin's 1997. 902. Biographical and bibliographical outline.

Deloux, Jean-Pierre, and others. "Le Dossier: Peter Straub, Polar et Fantastique." In *Polar* (Paris, France: Éditions Rivage) No. 19 (February 1998): 33-153. ISBN 2-7436-0333-X.
Special Peter Straub Issue, includes:
- Deloux, Jean-Pierre. "Un Fantastiquer Au Long Cours," pp. 33-49. Essay discussing Straub's work in general;
- Le Braz, François. "The Long Journey into Night," pp. 50-56. Examination of the Blue Rose sequence;
- Deloux, Jean-Pierre. "Le Livre des Mutations," pp. 57-60. Discussion of *The Hellfire Club;*
- Deloux, Jean-Pierre, and Jean-Paul Gratias. "Entretien Avec Peter Straub" 61-78. Interview with Straub;
- Deloux, Jean-Pierre. "Bibliographie," pp. 79-85; Gratias, Jean-Paul, translator. "Pork Pie Hat," pp. 86-153 [see B21].

Gagne, Paul. "An Interview with Peter Straub." *American Fantasy* No 1 (February 1982): 8-26.

Geddie, Tom. "Peter Straub: Interview." *Fantasy Newsletter* #46 (March 1982): 18-23.

Gregory, Jay. "TZ Interview: Peter Straub." *Twilight Zone Magazine* (May 1981): 13-16.

Guran, Paula. "*DarkEcho* Interview". *DarkEcho* Horror Web. June 1997. At: http://www.darkecho.com/darkecho/archives/straub.html.

Hickok, Andree. "Peter Straub: Master of Horror." (Bridgeport CT) *Sunday Post* 24 April 1983: E1, E8.

Hopkins, Casey L. "An Interview with Peter Straub." *Horror Literature Spotlight.* April 1996. Available at: http://www.drcasey.com/literature/spotlight/straub1.shtml. Online interview.

"Horror Panel I &II." *The Dick Cavett Show.* WNET, New York, 1980. Interview/Discussion with Straub, King, and George Romero.

Hughes, David, and Nick Belcher. "Straub: Eerie Fields Forever?" *Skeleton Crew* vol. 2, no 1 (July 1990): 6+. Interview.

Kendrick, Walter. *The Thrill of Fear: 250 Years of Scary Entertainment.* New York: Grove Weidenfeld, 1991. 255. Notes that "A Few novelists [in the years after 1970] also achieved mass success with straight-out horror: Stephen King became an institution, while Anne Rice, Clive Barker, and Peter Straub won critical recognition along with popularity."

Kennedy, Brian. "Frightmasters: Horror Authors on the Web." 23 April 1999. Available at: http://www.netguide.com/Snapshot/Archive?guide=entertainment&id=739. Online interview.

King, Stephen. "Peter Straub: An Informal Appreciation." *World Fantasy Convention '82.* Edited by Kennedy Poyser. New Haven CT: The Eighth World Fantasy Convention, 1982. 30 +. Straub is "simply the best writer of supernatural tales that I know. He has built upon things he has already done...but he has never repeated himself..." (31).

Macabre, J. B. "Shadows." *Fear!* #16 (April 1990): 24+. Interview; British publication.

McDonald, Thomas Liam. "Profiles in Terror: Peter Straub." *Cemetery Dance* vol. 3, no. 1 (Winter 1991): 16+; vol. 3, no. 2 (Spring 1991): 16+. Interview.

Meyer, Adam. "If You Could See Him Now: An Interview with Peter Straub." *Pirate Writings* vol. 3, #3, No. 8 (1995): 34+.

Michael Berry. *Horror* No. I (January 1994): 91. Interview. At: http://circle.greyware.com/people/MBerry/finger1.htm.

Neilson, Keith. "Contemporary Horror Fiction." *Horror Literature: A Reader's Guide.* Edited by Neil Barron. New York: Garland, 1990. 303-304.

New York Times 20 May 1979: VII, 56.

New York Times 27 April 1979: III, 28.

O'Brien, Maureen, and others. "Hot Deals." *Publishers Weekly* Vol. 240,No. 46 (15 December 1993): 24.

"Peter Straub." *Contemporary Authors.* Volumes 85-88. Edited by Frances Carol Locher. Detroit MI: Gale Research Company, The Book Tower, 1980.

"Peter Straub." *Contemporary Authors: New Revision Series.* Volume 28. Detroit MI: Gale Research, The Book Tower, 1990. 452-454.

"Peter Straub." *Contemporary Literary Criticism.* Vol. 28. Edited by Jean C. Stine. Detroit MI: Gale Research Company Book Tower, 1984. 408-412. Bio-critical reference article.

"Peter Straub." *Current Biography.* Vol. 50, No 2 (February 1989).

"Peter Straub: Seeing Double." *Locus* Vol. 41, No. 6, Issue 455 (December 1998). Interview. Excerpted: http://locusmag.com/Issues/1998/12/Straub.html

"Peter Straub: Interview." Interview. *The Armchair Detective* Vol. 27, No. 3, (Summer 1994).

Reader Advisory Services, County of Los Angeles Public Library. "Horror/Occult Grandmasters." 1996. Available at: http://www.colapublib.org/advisory/horror/master.html. Includes Straub on a "recommended" list with Clive Barker, Robert Bloch, Ramsey Campbell, Shirley Jackson, Stephen King, Dean R. Koontz, Robert McCammon, Dan Simmons, Bram Stoker, Whitley Strieber, Chelsea Quinn Yarbro, and others.

Schweitzer, Darrell. "A Talk with Peter Straub." *Worlds of Fantasy & Horror* Vol. 1, no. 14 (Winter 1996): 39+. Interview.

Searles, Baird, Beth Mecham, and Michael Franklin. "Peter Straub." *A Reader's Guide to Fantasy.* New York: Facts on File, 1982. 112-113.

Simmons, Wm. Mark. "The Quintessential 'Terrorist': A Chat with Peter Straub." *FrightNet Online Magazine* Issue 12 (April-May 1999). Available at: http://www.frightnet.con.

Skarda, Patricia L. "Peter Straub." *Dictionary of Literary Biography Yearbook: 1984.* Edited by Jean W. Ross. Detroit MI: Gale Research/Book Tower, 1985. Bio-critical reference article.

Skarda, Patricia. "Peter Straub (1943-). *The Penguin Encyclopedia of Horror and the Supernatural.* Edited by Jack Sullivan. New York: Viking, 1986. 406-408. Reference article.

Sullivan, Jack. "Breaking In: Peter Straub." *Twilight Zone* Vol. 6, No. 1 (April 1986): 26+. Biographical article.

Turner, Craig. "Peter Straub: Tales from the Shadowland." *Exuberance* no. 3 (1991): 28+. Article; British magazine.

Wiater, Stanley, and Roger Anker. Interview with Stephen King and Peter Straub. 1984 World Fantasy Convention, Ottawa Canada.

Wiater, Stanley, and Roger Anker. "Titans of Terror." *Valley Advocate* 31

October 1984: 1, A9-A10.

Wiater, Stanley, and Roger Anker. Interview with Stephen King and Peter Straub. Rpt in: *Fangoria* #42 (February 1985); # 43 (March 1985).

Wiater, Stanley, and Roger Anker. Interview with Stephen King and Peter Straub. Rpt. as a portion of: Chapter Five: "Partners in Fear." *Bare Bones: Conversations on Terror with Stephen King*. Edited by Tim Underwood and Chuck Miller. [See entry for 1988, below]

Wiater, Stanley. "Interview: Peter Straub." *Fangoria* #16 (August, 1981).

Wiater, Stanley. Interview with Peter Straub. *Valley Advocate,* February 23, 1987.

Wiater, Stanley. "Interview: Peter Straub." *New Blood,* (Fall 1988). Rpt. of interview "When Lightning Strikes" in *Fear* #1.

Wiater, Stanley. "Interview with Peter Straub." *Science Fiction Media* #60, May 1989. Munich, Germany. Rpt. of interview "When Lightning Strikes" in *Fear* #1.

Wiater, Stanley. "Stephen King and Peter Straub." *Dark Dreamers: Conversattions with the Masters of Horror,* Avon Books, 1990. Excerpted as: Stephen King and Peter Straub." *Altered Earth Arts Portfolio #7.* Available at:
http://www.alteredearth.com/wiater/king.htm.

Wiater, Stanley. "When Lightning Strikes." *Fear!* #1 (July/August 1988): 58+. Interview; first issue of the British magazine.

Wiater, Stanley. Chapter Five: "Partners in Fear." *Bare Bones: Conversations on Terror with Stephen King,* edited by Tim Underwood and Chuck Miller. Los Angeles, CA, Columbia, PA: Underwood-Miller, 1988, 259 p., cloth, pp. 153-180. Limited edition of 1,000 copies, numbered. Three interviews with Straub and Stephen King from 1979 through 1984.

• Los Angeles, CA, Columbia, PA: Underwood-Miller, 1988, 259 p., limited edition, lettered A-ZZ, bound in leather.

• Los Angeles, CA, Columbia, PA: Underwood-Miller, 1988, 259 p., presentation copies, 100 copies.

• New York: McGraw-Hill, 1988, x+211 p., cloth. 153-180. ISBN 0-07-065759-9. New York: Warner Books, 1989, July 1989, x+211 p., trade paper.

• As: *Angst. Gespräche Über das Unheimliche mit Stephen King.* Linkenheim, Germany: Edition Phantasia, 1989, 368 pp., DM 148, 330 numbered copies, 30 numbered I-XXX. German translation by Joachim Körber. ISBN 3-924959-32-3

• London: New English Library, 1989, 217 p., cloth. London: New English Library, 1990, 217 p., paper.

Wiater, Stanley. Interview with Stephen King and Peter Straub. 1979 World Fantasy Convention, Providence RI. *Springfield Morning Union* 31 Oct 1979.

Wiater, Stanley. Interview with Stephen King and Peter Straub. 1980 World Fantasy Convention, Baltimore MD. *Valley Advocate* 8 April 1981; 27 May 1981.

Wiater, Stanley. Interview with Stephen King and Peter Straub. *Fangoria* #6 (June 1980).

Wiater, Stanley. Interview with Stephen King and Peter Straub. Rpt. as a portion of: Chapter Five: "Partners in Fear." *Bare Bones: Conversations on Terror with Stephen King*. Edited by Tim Underwood and Chuck Miller. [See entry for 1988, below]

Wiater, Stanley. Interview with Stephen King and Peter Straub. Rpt. as a portion of: Chapter Five: "Partners in Fear." *Bare Bones: Conversations on Terror with Stephen King*. Edited by Tim Underwood and Chuck Miller. [See entry for 1988, below]

Winter, Douglas E. "Creating *Koko*: A Conversation with Peter Straub. *Twilight Zone* Vol. 8, No. 6 (February 1989): 26+. Interview.

Winter, Douglas E. "Peter Straub." *Faces of Fear*. New York: Berkeley, 1985. Interview.
  • London: Pan, July 1990, 334 pp., £3.99, paperback. 271-286. Cover art by Dave McKean. ISBN 0-330-31246-4.

Winter, Douglas. "Stephen King, Peter Straub, and the Quest for 'The Talisman.'" *Twilight Zone* (January/February 1985). Interview.

Winter, Douglas. *Stephen King: The Art of Darkness*. New York: NAL, 1984, 252 pp., $14.95, hardcover. 2, 12, 29, 108, 138-150, 155, 164, 185, 187, 195-196, 210-212. ISBN 0-453-00476-8.

Acknowledgements

I appreciate the willing assistance of a number of people in compiling this bibliography, including Peter Straub; Michael Heppne (International editions); Benoit Domis and Daniel Conrad (France); Vanessa Marchand (France); and Hans-Ake Lilja (Sweden). In addition, I am grateful to Dave Hinchberger of Overlook Connection Press for his encouragement and support; and to my family for their eternal patience.

Index

[Note: Secondary sources listed alphabetically by surname in Section G
do not appear in this Index.]

"45 Calibrations of Raymond Chandler": C16
"A Loosening, A Spending Prose: A2, A11, D13
"A Short Guide to the City": A16, B14
"A Triple-Decker Novel: A11, D45
"After the Return": A3, D32
"Ashputtle": B19
 "Author's Note": A16, C6
"Blue Rose": A14, A16, B5
"Bunjee Jumping Without a Cord, Plus Some Comments on Style" :
    C20
"Circling the Ground": A3, D18
"Coming to One": A3, D34
"Coming to Rest": A11, D50
"Downtown, Way Down: A2, A11, D10
"Encantadas": A11, D41
"Envoi From A Brother": A2, A11, D15
"Explications": A3, D24
"Facing Land's End": A11, D44
"Facing the Lavish Weather": A11, D43
"Fee": B20
"For Ann Lauterbach": A11, D48
"For Thomas Tessier": A11, D57
"Fox by the Pool": A3, D23
"Fox in Snow": A3, D17
"Fox Reading": A3, D20
"Fox Survives": A3, D16
"Fox's Address to the Delegates" A3, D21
"Fox's Arrogance" : A3, D22
"From Lawrence's Letters: A2, A11, D14
"From Mrs. God": A16, A17, B4, B12
"From the Heian Court": A11, D49
"Hunger: An Introduction" : F5
"Hunger: An Introduction": A20, B22
"In Transit": B23
"Interlude: Bar Talk:" A 16, B7

"Interlude: Going Home": A16, B8

"Interlude: In the Realm of Dreams": A16, B9

"Interlude: The Poetry Reading": A16, B10

"Interlude: The Veteran": A16, B11

"Introduction": C2, C3, C4, C6, C11, C12, C15, C18

"Ishmael in Manhattan: A2, A11, D9

"Ishmael's Song to His Sister: A2, A11, D8

"Isn't It Romantic?": B25

"Isobel's Recitative": A3, D31

"Lessive": A11, D55

"Lichens": A11, D53

"Looking Back": C22

"Making the Circle's Figure: Five French Poems": A11, D42

"Meeting Stevie": C1

"Mr. Clubb and Mr. Cuff": B24, F5

"Mrs. God": A16, A17, B4, B12

"Muhammed's Song": A3, D27

"My Life in Pictures": A1, A11, D1

"MYSTERY, Mystery, and Mystery Novels" : C8

"On Hampstead Heath with Women: A2, A11, D6

"On Mortality and Change: Afterword":C9

"Photographic Plate": A11, D51

"Pork Pie Hat": B21

"Preparations for Dying": A3, D30

"Reading the Well": A11, D47

"Ringing the Changes," by Robert Aickman: C7

"Routine Teuton": B2

"Sentences for Rimbaud": A11, D56

"She Saw a Young Man": A16, B13

"Something about Death, Something about a Fire": A16, B15

"Song for One on Water: A2, A11, D12

"Stephen King: *The Shining*": C5

"Text": A11, D58

"The Blessing": A3, D33

"The Bow: A2, A11, D3

"The Buffalo Hunter": A16, B6

"The Cloak," by Robert Bloch: C12

"The Desert Motion": A2, A11, D2

"The Fantasy of Everyday Life": C21

"The Fifties" : C10

"The Figures on the Beach": A11, D46

"The First Bedouin": A2, A11, D7
"The Ghost Village": B18
"The Juniper Tree": A16, B3
"The Kingdom of Heaven": B17
"The Music He Hears: A2, A11, D11
"The One, The Only R. C., Then, Now, and Forever": C13
"The Sleepers: A2, A11, D5
"The Trace": A11, D54
"Then One Day She Saw Him Again": A16, B16
"Tracking": A3, D19
"Using the Bow: A2, A11, D4
"Various Encounters with Karl": C17
"William F. Nolan: An Introduction": C14
"Withstanding, Saving, Moving": A11, D52
"Wolf and the Territory": A3, D29
"Wolf on the Plains": A3, D25
"Wolf's Litany": A3, D28
"Words from the Island": A3, D26
1997 Dark Progress, Horror Writers Calendar: F3
A Sailboat in the Moonlight [recording]: E1
Ackroyd, Peter: A6
Adams Round Table: B25
Adams, Leith: C10
Adams, Phoebe-Lou: A7
Adler, Constance: A12
After Hours [recording]: E15
Aguirre, Manuel: A7
Aickman, Robert: C4, C7
All Bird's Children [recording] : E8
Amantia, A. M. B. : A12
Amblin Entertainment: A12
Anders, Smiley: A12
Annichiario, Mark: A21
Are You Loathsome Tonight?, by Poppy Z. Brite: C18
Armless Maiden, The, edited by Terri Windling: B3
Barker, Clive: B3
Barth, John: F1
Beagle, Peter: A12
Beahm, George: A12
Black Thorn, White Rose, edited by Ellen Datlow and Terri Windling:
   B19

Bloch, Robert: C12, F1
Blue Rose: A14
Blue, Tyson: A12, A20
Borderlands 4, edited by Thomas Monteleone F.: B20
Borst, Ronald V.: C10
Bosky, Bernadette: A12
Bradbury, Ray: A2, F1
Braffa Ruby: E1
Bram Stoker Best Novel Award, Horror Writers of America: A19
Bred Any Good Books Lately?, edited by James Charlton: B2
Breque, Jean-Daniel: A10
Brief Lives, by Neil Gaiman: C9
Brite, Poppy Z.: C18
British Fantasy Award: A9
Bryant, Edward: A20, A21, F3
Bryden, Ronald: A4
Burns, Keith: C10
Cady, Jack: B3
Campbell, Dan G.: A15, A16
Campbell, Ramsey: B3, C5, C13, F1
Casey, Carol K: A6
Chandler, Raymond: C16
Chandler, Stacy Brown: A21
Charlton, James: B2
Cheuse, Alan: A12
Chow, Dan: A15, A16, A17
Clark, Leigh: F3
Clark, Theresa J: A12
Clegg, Douglas: F3
Clooney, Rosemary: E6
Collings, Michael R: A12, A16
Collins, Robert A. : A9
Core of Ramsey Campbell, The, by Ramsey Campbell: C13
Cortland, Will: A12
Cunningham, Valentine: A5, A7
D'Ammassa, Don: A20
D'Angelo, John: A12
Dameron, Ned: A14
Dark Voices, edited by Stephen Jones and Clarence Paget: C7
Datlow, Ellen: B19
De Lint, Charles: A15

DeHaven, Tom: A21
Devereux, Robert: F3
Dorey, Alan: A9
Double Exposure [recording] : E4
Dunn, Katherine: A21
Dziemianowicz, Stephen: A15, C13
Eaglen, Audrey: A12
Easy Going [recording]: E5
Eidus, Janice: A13
Electronic Poetry Center: F5
Etchison, Dennis: A2, A14, B3, B18, F1
Exorcisms and Ecstasies, by Karl Edward Wagner: C17
Faust, Christa: F3
Fazell, Daryl: A12
Fear Itself, edited by Tim Underwood and Chuck Miller: C1
Flagan, Tommy: E16
Floating Dragon: A9
Frane, Jeff: A2
Freedman, Richard: A9
Full Circle. See *Julia*: A5
Fuller, Edmund: A7
Fuller, Richard: A15
Gaiman, Neil: C9
General's Wife, The: A10, C2. See also "The General's Wife": B1, C2.
Ghost Story: A7
Ghosts, Peter Straub's. See *Peter Straub's Ghosts,* A20
Goldstein, William: A12
Gordon, James: A5
Gordon, Jon: E9
Graeber, Laurel: A16, A19
Grant, Charles L.: B3
Graven Images, edited by Ronald V. Borst, Keith Burns, and Leith Adams: C10
Great Writers and Their Kids Write Spooky Stories, edited by Martin Greenberg, Jill M. Morgan, and Robert Weinberg: B23
Greenberg, Lawrence: A20
Greenberg, Martin: B23, C22
Grooms, Roger: A12
Guran, Paula: A21
Hamilton, Scott: E1, E3, E7, E11, E15
Harrison, Colin: A21

Harrison, M. John: B3
Hartmann, Roland: B21
Harvey, L. J.: A12
Hazel, Paul: B3
Heaven [recording]: E2
Helleny, Joe: E13
Hellfire Club, The: A21
Hemesath, James E: A8, A9
Herbert, Frank: A12
Herron, Don: A12
Hill, Douglas: A7
Hillerman, Tony: F1
Hinckley, Barbara: A7
Hinckley, Karen: A7
Hoffert, Barbara: A21
Horror: 100 Best Books, edited by Stephen Jones and Kim Newman:
    C5
Houses without Doors: A16, C6
If You Could See Me Now: A6. See also *Wild Animals*: A13
In a Lonely Place, by Karl Edward Wagner: C3
International Conference on the Fantastic in the Arts: C21, F4
Into the Woods: The Best of Phil Woods: E12
Irish University Press: A3
Ishmael: A2
Island of Dr. Moreau, The, by H. G. Wells: C15
Jaffe, Nora Crow: A7
John Gordon Quartet: E9
Johnson, Eric W. : A13
Johnson, George: A15
Jones, Stephen: C5, C7
Joshi, S. T.: C1
Julia: A5. See also *Wild Animals*: A13
Kadet, Gary: A21
Kaganoff, P. : A18
Keates, Jonathan: A6
Kendrick, Walter: A16
Kenney, Peter: A21
Kernan, Michael: A12
Key, Samuel M. : A18
King of the Cats. See *Shadowland*: A8
King, Stephen : A2, A7, A12, B3, F1; *The Talisman*: A12

Kirk, Robin: A12
Klett, Rex: B25
Koger, Grove: A7
Koja, Kathe: A20
Koko: A15
Le Guin, Ursula K.: F1
Leerhsen, Charles: A12
Leeson Park and Belsize Square: Poems 1970-1975: A11
Lehmann-Haupt, Christopher: A7, A8, A9, A12, A16, A21
Levin, Martin: A4
Lewis, Don: A12
Liberatore, Karen: A12
Ligotti, Thomas: B3
Lileks, James: A12
Linaweaver, Brad: A20
Lip Service [recording]: E13
Lochte, Dick: A9
Lord John Signatures: F1
Lucas, Tim: A5, A7
Lyons, Gene: A7, A19
MacCulloch, Simon: A21
Magic Terror: A25
Magistrale, Tony: A12
Mainhardt, Ricia: C12
Make a Wish Foundation: F3
Mance, Junior: E10
Marriages: A4.
Mason, Michael: A5
Matheson, Richard: C12
Matthews, Barbara: A8
McC.Dresser, Sheila: A12
McGrath, Patrick: B17
McLaurin, Preston: A12
Meinert, Renald: A7
Mellors, John: A5
Merritt, Robert: A12
MetaHorror, edited by Dennis Etchison: B18
Miller, Chuck: A12, C1
Miller, Faren: A12, A16, A18
Millhiser, Marlys: A12
Monteleone, Thomas F. : A20, B20

Montiglio, Steve: F3
Morgan, Jill M. : B23, C22
Morrell, David: B3
Morrison, Michael: A14, A15
Morrow, Bradford: B17
Mothers & Sons, edited by Jill Morgan and Martin Greenberg: C22
Mr. X: A24
Mrs. God: A17
Mulligan, Gerry: E3
Murder for Halloween, edited by Michele Slung and Roland Hartman:
    B21
Murder for Revenge, edited by Otto Penzler: B24
Murder on the Run, edited by the Adams Round Table: B25
My Life in Pictures A1
Mystery: A18
Nathan, Paul: A8, A12, A18
Navarro, Yvonne: F3
Neilson, Keith: A5, A6, A7, A8, A9, A11
Newman, Kim: C5
Nicholls, Peter: A7
Night Shapes, by William F. Nolan: C14
Nolan, William F.: C14, F3
Norton, Nik: A15
Oates, Joyce Carol: F1
Open Air: A3
Paget, Clarence: C7
Pallamary, Matthew J. : F3
Partridge, Norman: A20
Penzler, Otto: B24
People Online Conference: C19
Peplowski, Ken: E4
Perret, Patti: F2
Perry, Clark: A20
Perry, Pamela M: A12
Peter and PTR: A22
Peter Straub's Ghosts: A20
Phil Woods Quintet: E3, E8, E12
Pollack, Dale: A12
Pork Pie Hat: A23
Prime Evil, edited by Douglas E. Winter: B3
Radio City [recording]: E7

Reagan, Reilly: A19
Reino, Joseph: A12
Relling, William, Jr. : F3
Rems, Jack: A2
Reuter, Madalynne: A12
Richmond, Peter: A12
Ridge, Putney Tyson, Ph.D. (pseudonym for Straub): A4, A5, A6, A7, A8, A9, A15, A16, A17, A18, A19, A20, A21
Righton, Barbara: A7, A9
Robert Bloch, edited by Richard Matheson and Ricia Mainhardt: C12
Rodgers, Alan: A20
Ross, Gordon R.: A20
Rothenstein, Richard: A12
Rückbeil, Andrea: A7
Ryan, John: A6, A9
Saidman, Anne: A12
Sammon, Paul M.: A20
Sanders, Joe: A12, A13
Sandman, The, by Neil Gaiman: C9
Schachtsiek-Freitag, Norbert: A12
Schlobin, Roger: A9
Schow, David G. : F3
Schulman, Madeline G: A5
Schulte, Jean: A12
Schuyler, William W., Jr. : A15
Schweitzer, Darrell: A12
Scott Hamilton Quintet: E7
Scott Hamilton with Strings [recording]: E11
Seafront Press: A1
Shadowland: A8
Shapiro, Anna: A12
Shepard, Lucius: A15
Sherman, David: A12
Show Tunes [recording]: E6
Silva, David B. : A20
Simmons, Dan: F1
Skarda, Patricia: A7
Skow, John: A12
Slay, Jack, Jr. : A12
Slung, Michelle: B21
Small, Michael: A12

Smith, Kristen L: A7

Smith, Tim: A20

Smithers, Susan L. : A12

Soft Lights & Sweet Music [recording]: E3

Somerville, Richard: A12

Spielberg, Steven: A12

Spignesi, Stephen J. : A12

Steinberg, Sylvia: A12, A13, A15, A16, A18, A19, A21

Stout, Rex: C11

Straub, Benjamin: B23

Stuewe, Paul: A12

Sullivan, Jack: A7

Suttcliffe, Thomas: A8

Talisman, The [with Stephen King]: A12

Talk to Me Baby [recording]: E14

Taylor, Lucy: F3

Terrell, Carroll F.: A12

Tessier, Thomas: A1, B3

Faces of Fantasy, The, photographs by Patti Perret: F2

Sunset and the Mockingbird, The [recording]: E16

Throat, The: A19, F5

Toepfer, Susan: A12

Tommy Flagan Trio: E16

Too Many Cooks, by Rex Stout: C11

Tucker, Ken: A12

Turner, Billy: A12

Turret Books: A2

Under Venus. See *Wild Animals*: A13

Underwood, Tim: A12, C1

Updike, John: F1

Vache, Warren: E5, E14

Wagner, Hank: A7

Wagner, Karl Edward: C3, C17

Wallace, Gail Smith: A12

Wallace, Jon: A19

Walters, Ray: A7

Walton, David: A21

Weinberg, Robert: B23

Wells, H. G. : C15

Westlake, Donald E.: F1

Whitley Strieber: B3

Wild Animals—Three Novels: A13
Wilkinson, Joanne: A21
Williamson, Chet: A20
Wilson, Frank: A19
Windling, Terri: B3, B19
Wine-Dark Sea, The, by Robert Aickman: C4
Winnett, Scott: B17
Winter, Douglas E. : A6, A12, A13, B3, F3
Wolfe, Gene: B17
Woods, Phil: E2, E8, E12
World Fantasy Award: A8, A12, A15, B18
World Horror 2000: F6
World Horror Award: B24

www.ingramcontent.com/pod-product-compliance
Lightning Source LLC
Chambersburg PA
CBHW030334030726
47499CB00003B/775